"You told me you don't like to be in one place too long," Marianne said.

Ridge noticed that she was watching him intently. "You miss things that way."

"Such as?"

He shrugged. "Friends. Dogs. Having a place to come back to at the end of the day that doesn't charge you when you walk in the door."

He could tell she hadn't expected that. "You like Harland, then?"

"Very much." There was plenty to like about the close-knit community on and around the farm. Because Ridge didn't know how to say that without spooking her, he settled on something less personal. "Little things mean a lot when you don't have them."

She eyed him with something resembling respect, which he took as a good sign. Marianne was by far the most mistrustful woman he'd ever met.

He still wasn't sure why he was trying so hard to get through to her, and he had to wonder if his genetic stubbornness was steering him down a rocky, dead-end road.

Books by Mia Ross

Love Inspired

Hometown Family
Circle of Family

MIA ROSS

loves great stories. She enjoys reading about fascinating people, long-ago times and exotic places. But only for a little while, because her reality is pretty sweet. Married to her college sweetheart, she's the proud mom of two amazing kids, whose schedules keep her hopping. Busy as she is, she can't imagine trading her life for anyone else's—and she has a pretty good imagination. You can visit her online at www.miaross.com.

Circle of Family

Mia Ross

Love Inspired

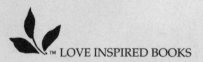

™ LOVE INSPIRED BOOKS

Recycling programs
for this product may
not exist in your area.

ISBN-13: 978-0-373-81647-7

CIRCLE OF FAMILY

www.LoveInspiredBooks.com

Printed in U.S.A.

Let all that you do be done in love.
—*1 Corinthians* 16:14

For my friends who had the courage
to make a new life for themselves and their children.
I admire you more than I can say.

Acknowledgments

To the pros who helped me make this book exactly
what it should be: Elaine Spencer, Melissa Endlich,
Rachel Burkot and the very talented staff
at Love Inspired.

A high five to all the dedicated—and very patient—
coaches my children have had over the years.
The hours are long and the weather can be awful,
but you've had a tremendous impact on them.
It really does take a village to raise a child, and
I know my kids are better people because of you.

More thanks to the gang at Seekerville
(www.seekerville.net). You give me
a place to share good news and bad,
and I always leave with a smile on my face.

As always, this book didn't get written in a closet.
My friends and family surround me with support
and encouragement every single day.
I couldn't possibly do this without you.

Chapter One

"What in the world?"

Up to her elbows in pink ribbons and last-minute wedding favors, Marianne Weston looked around the decorated yard to find the source of a persistent drone that was getting louder by the second. When she realized it was coming from overhead, she glanced up at the cloudless sky. The sound seemed to be racing the midmorning sun, and she shaded her eyes to look toward the east. Squinting against the sunlight, she saw a blue-and-yellow biplane barreling toward the Sawyer family farm.

So low it had to be clipping the trees, she thought for sure the plane was going to crash in the front hayfield. As she watched in amazement, it soared no more than six feet over the large white farmhouse, rocking its wings as if the maneuver was an everyday occurrence. It made a graceful loop before coming in to land in a fallow cornfield.

After that, nothing. She wasn't close enough to see what the pilot was doing, but she knew he had to be her brother Matt's best man. She'd never met Ridge Collins, and something told her this wouldn't be your run-of-the-mill introduction.

Marianne put out the last of the ribbon-tied candy bags and headed up to welcome him. Several chickadees chattered at her from their home in one of the eaves as she passed by the flower-draped front porch. She strolled up the gentle slope, assessing the situation as she went. Life had taught her to be cautious, but the man's unusual appearance had definitely piqued her curiosity.

Just as she topped the rise, the pilot popped up from his seat like a jack-in-the-box, his boots clanging as he descended the ladder attached to the side of the plane. Bracing his hand on the side, he looked underneath, then stepped back and folded his arms. After a few seconds, he was apparently satisfied.

"Thanks for a quick ride, girl," he said, patting the plane as if it were a horse who'd just given him a good run. "I'm late, so your rubdown will have to wait."

The man talked to his plane, Marianne thought with a smile. No wonder Matt had never introduced him to the family.

As she approached, she wasn't sure how to greet him, so she went with something light. "That was quite a landing."

When he turned to face her, her heart skipped a couple of beats. When it started up again, she had to remind herself to breathe.

He looked like he'd just stepped out of *Pearl Harbor,* one of her favorite movies. His battered leather jacket had a faded animal on the front, and his threadbare jeans had seen much better days. Mirrored aviator sunglasses completed the image. She could almost hear sweeping orchestra music welcoming the hero home.

A friend from Matt's wilder days, Ridge held himself with relaxed confidence. Rugged and independent, he was handsome in a rough-and-tumble kind of way. While they stood looking at each other, Marianne wondered how many women had lost their hearts to this man.

Fortunately, logic returned and set her back on her usual even keel. Intriguing as this man might be, she wasn't one to blindly follow her heart anymore. Her ex-husband had cured her of her romantic streak a long time ago.

It wasn't exactly the reception he'd expected.

According to Matt, his tiny North Carolina hometown was full of gossips and busybodies but was the sort of place that greeted everyone with open arms. Even during the years he'd avoided his sad memories of home, Matt had told him how friendly and open his family was.

So Ridge felt a little awkward standing there while this very pretty woman studied him like a specimen on a tray. The breeze ruffled her honey-gold hair, and her icy-blue eyes stared him down like a gunfighter's. Then he realized he was still wearing his sunglasses.

He dropped them to hang from their braided cord and smiled as he offered his hand. "Ridge Collins."

She took his hand without hesitation, but he got the feeling her smile was a bit forced. "Marianne Weston. Welcome to Harland."

It was the kind of tone people reserved for annoying salesmen, but Ridge did his best to ignore it. He was later than he'd promised, after all, and he hadn't called. In his experience, women hated it when he made excuses.

"Sorry I'm late. The weather got kinda nasty west of here."

"You put on quite a show coming in that way," she said as a screen door slammed.

Ridge glanced at the house to find two kids headed their way. The boy was in a gray suit, complete with navy tie. Wearing a pouf of a pink dress, the little girl made him think of a sugarplum fairy. Freshly scrubbed and polished, they looked ready for a wedding. Too bad he didn't, he chided himself. Then Marianne might have been a little happier to see him.

"A big part of my business is aerial tours," he explained. "Folks love to see what the old girl can do."

"Do they?"

Her brittle tone sent up a red flag, and he back-pedaled like a center fielder at Yankee Stadium. "Some of 'em."

She nailed him with a glare. "You scared me half to death, skimming over my house like that."

"I apologize. I left a big buffer, but it must've looked closer from the ground."

Based on her peeved look, he'd expected more of a lashing. Something apparently changed her mind, though, and her disapproval melted into a beautiful smile. The difference was striking, and he wished he knew which button he'd just pushed. He wouldn't mind seeing that smile again.

"No harm done, I guess. I'm just glad you got here safely." She motioned toward the boy standing a respectful couple of feet away. "This is my son, Kyle, and this—" she held an arm out to the adorable princess "—is Emily. Kids, this is Mr. Collins."

"Ridge is fine." Reaching out, he shook Kyle's hand before hunkering down in front of Emily to avoid towering over her. Offering his hand, he grinned. "Your Uncle Matt's told me a lot about you. It's nice to finally meet you guys."

Emily was a miniature version of her mother, and she assessed him with a curious look as she shook his hand. "Ridge is kind of a funny name."

Marianne clicked her tongue, but Ridge chuckled. "Actually, it's worse than that. My mom named me for Breckenridge, Colorado, the town we were living in when I was born." He saw Kyle edging closer, and he glanced up at him. "Good thing we weren't living in Albuquerque, huh?" he added with a wink.

The kid responded with a gap-toothed grin, then looked pointedly at the plane. "How come your plane has *Betsy* written on it?"

"She's named for my grandmother."

"Why?"

"Well, it was kind of a wreck when Grandpa brought it home. He named it after her so she wouldn't kill him."

"What's this?" Emily asked, pointing at the front of his jacket.

"A wolf." He shifted to show her the full-size version on the back. "My great-grandfather flew in the Wolf Pack in World War Two."

"Is this his plane?" Kyle asked, eyes wide with amazement.

"No, but it's the same kind he trained in."

Kyle opened his mouth for another question, but his mother cut him off. "I'm sure Mr. Collins is tired from his trip. Why don't we bring him inside and get him something to eat?"

The mother-hen comment made him remember something. "That sounds great, but I have to make a call first." He swept a hand in Betsy's general direction. "Go ahead and have a look."

The kids didn't have to be asked twice, and he enjoyed watching them gawk at his pride and joy. When he caught Marianne frowning at the plane, he assumed she was angry with him for landing at the farm. With the wedding only a couple of hours away, he understood.

"Matt said it was okay to fly in here," he said. "But I can head to the airstrip outside of town if you'd rather."

"No, it's fine." Sighing, she shook her head. "When your response card said you were bringing Betsy, I thought she was your date."

At first, he didn't get it. When the significance of the misunderstanding hit him, he felt terrible. "And you ordered her a meal."

"There was no food preference, so I went with the chicken."

A laugh was threatening, but she seemed like the serious type, and he didn't want to insult her. "Sorry about that. I figured Matt would know I was flying out here."

After a second, humor warmed her eyes to the color of a flawless summer sky. "I guess I should've chosen high-test."

They both laughed, and he was relieved that their awkward first meeting had turned into something more positive.

"Excuse me a minute." He took his cell phone from the pocket of his jeans. When Marianne started to move away, he waved her back. "No need to leave. Mom was worried about the weather, so I promised to call her when I landed."

He punched up her number and waited for the call to connect.

"Your mother is number one on your speed dial?" Marianne asked.

He chuckled. "She wouldn't have it any other way. Hey, there. Yeah, I'm fine." He paused, then chuckled again. "Yes, I'm telling the truth. Okay, hang on."

Holding up the phone, he snapped a picture of himself in front of Betsy and hit Send. While he waited for the picture message to go through, he sighed. He loved his mom to pieces, but she worried about him way too much. For her birthday, he'd gotten her a cute fox terrier to dote on, but it hadn't changed anything. He still flew, and she still worried. It was kind of comforting, in a way. No matter how old he got, he'd always be her boy.

"Believe me now? Good. Give your little ankle biter a treat for me." He grinned. "Love you more. See you in a couple weeks."

He hit the off button and noticed Marianne's expression. Since he'd just met her, he couldn't be sure about it, but she seemed to like what she'd heard. "Moms. What can you do?"

"We are what we are."

"I'm real sorry I didn't call to tell you about my change in plans," Ridge apologized again.

She waved it away as she took Emily's hand and turned toward the house. "We're used to it."

As he followed Marianne and the kids inside—carrying his duffel bag and suit carrier—Ridge admired the setting for his best friend's wedding. The garden out front was magazine-perfect, with a rose-covered trellis and round tables scattered around the expansive side yard. Each one was draped in linen and held a vase overflowing with flowers. There were several racks covered in tarps. He assumed they were for the folding chairs, and he made a mental note to help put them away later.

With the kind of efficiency that came from lots of practice, Marianne pulled out snacks and juice boxes, then set glasses and a pitcher of sweet tea on the table. Ridge decided it was best to get out what he wanted to say.

"Matt told me about your father passing last year. I'm so sorry."

"Thank you," she said as she'd probably done a million times since his sudden death. Her eyes went to the empty chair at the head of the table. "We really miss him."

Ridge wished he could say the same about his own father. Unfortunately, when the abusive drunk who'd made his childhood a living nightmare died a few years ago, it took every ounce of compassion he had not to celebrate.

While she sliced up some great-smelling banana bread, he filled glasses with ice and tea for both of them. After a long swallow, he grinned his appreciation. "I've been out west the last month. I really missed this stuff."

That got him a gracious smile. "There's always plenty, so help yourself."

"Southern hospitality," he complimented her as he refilled his glass. "Gotta love it."

"Don't get used to it, city boy."

Ridge glanced over to find Matt Sawyer filling the doorway. Dressed in a gray suit with a buttoned-up white shirt and burgundy tie, Matt looked a lot different from the last time Ridge had seen him. Of course, that had been a trip to Vegas he suspected Matt's family knew nothing about.

Laughing, Ridge shook his old buddy's hand.

"I won't, believe me. Betsy and I don't fare well if we're in one place too long."

Matt took the sweet tea Marianne handed him and drained it in three gulps. "Thanks, Mare."

"When did you finish up the haying last night?"

Matt squinted at the schoolhouse clock on the wall. "Two, I think. There's a lot more to do, but I've done all I can."

"We need some more help around here," she commented with a worried frown.

"Can't afford it. Speaking of help, that reminds me," he said to Ridge. "I rustled up some dusting contracts for you. Starting with us Monday morning. Did you talk to John?"

"Your little brother said I can stay with him while I'm in town. He was really cool about it."

"Not much bothers John." Matt glanced at his sister and apparently read the very obvious disdain on her face. "What?"

She didn't respond, just stood there with her arms folded and giving him The Look. After a few seconds, understanding dawned, and he chuckled. Ridge didn't remember Matt having much of a sense of humor, and he suspected the bride had something to do with his buddy's new lighthearted view of things.

"Forgot to tell you Ridge was staying here, didn't I?" Matt asked his sister.

"Yes."

"Sorry."

He leaned in to kiss her cheek, and she swatted him away with a laugh. "Since you're getting married today, I'll let it slide."

"Come on." Matt motioned Ridge toward the stairs. "I'll show you where to get ready."

As they went up the creaky wooden steps, Ridge said, "So, should I guess from what you were saying to Marianne that things are still pretty tight around here?"

"*Tight* ain't the word. We're better off than some, but not as good as I'd like."

Ridge knew Matt wouldn't accept anything more than free labor, but he resolved to find a way to help the Sawyers out a little. He wasn't exactly swimming in money himself, but maybe he could come up with something.

In the meantime, he could manufacture a pleasant distraction. "I flew over your new house on my way through town. It looks great."

"Yeah?" Matt opened the door at the end of the upstairs hallway. "I've been working so much, I haven't seen it in daylight since last week."

"The roof was going on." Ridge laid his suit carrier across the foot of the bed. "I like the siding. Who decided on light green?"

"We both did. Caty wanted yellow, I wanted blue, so we settled on green."

Just saying her name eased the tension from his voice, and Ridge congratulated himself on breaking Matt out of his funk.

"You're really happy, aren't you?" Ridge asked, even though he knew the answer. It was written all over the guy's face.

"Yeah." He added a wry grin. "Me and a lawyer. Who'd've figured on that?"

Ridge made a show of thinking that one over, and they both burst out laughing. It was a good start to the day.

The morning flew by in a blink and before Marianne knew it, she and Lisa were standing in their places waiting for Caty to come down the aisle. Refusing to choose between them, the bride had cleverly solved the problem by making them her "sisters of honor." Unconventional, but Marianne appreciated her coming up with a solution that wouldn't hurt anyone's feelings.

Angling a glance to her right, Marianne decided her little sister looked like a rosebud. They were wearing the same pink dress, but Lisa's chandelier earrings sparkled in the sunlight, and the tiny roses and baby's breath she'd eased into her French braid were the perfect touch.

After Emily skipped down the aisle and joined them, Marianne rested a hand on the bouncing flower girl's shoulder to keep her in one spot. The guitarist strummed the first chords of the wedding march, prompting everyone to stand and look expectantly toward the front porch.

There, beneath swags of roses and hibiscus, the bride smiled up at the father she hadn't even known a year ago. As they made their way toward the flower-draped arbor, Ridge tapped Matt's shoulder and leaned in to say something. Whatever it was made her brother grin like an idiot, and Marianne sent up a desperate plea for divine intervention in getting them to behave themselves for just ten more minutes. Since Matt was the oldest Sawyer, she'd never had much luck being a mother hen to him in the past. Still, miracles happened every day.

Like the one that had brought Matt and Caty together in the first place.

In the past year, they'd navigated a long, rough road. Now they stood in the same spot where her parents, Ethan and Jan Sawyer, were married thirty-five years ago. The couple repeated their vows back to Pastor Charles in clear, confident voices. Despite their obvious differences, Marianne believed with all her heart that they really were meant for each other.

She wished their parents had lived long enough to see Matt so happy.

A warm breeze rustled through the roses climbing over the archway, releasing the sweet scent of the pink-and-white blossoms to mix with the hyacinth and jasmine in the garden surrounding them. Fifty-three guests were there, smiling and snapping pictures from every angle. Today really was perfect, she thought with a smile. She couldn't have asked for anything more.

When Matt turned to Ridge for Caty's ring, Marianne's sunny mood took a sudden dive. The best man's crazy—and unexpected—arrival had put her more on edge than she needed to be. As if she didn't have enough to worry about, now she'd have a stranger wandering around the farm for the next two weeks until he headed back to Colorado. She'd get Matt for that one, she promised herself.

After less than a minute with Ridge, she'd pegged him as disorganized and cocky. Although she had to admit the phone call to his mom had netted him some points. A grown man who so obviously loved his mother couldn't be all bad.

And no woman with a pulse could help noticing that his tall, solid frame looked as good in his crisp gray suit as it had in jeans and a leather bomber jacket. Or that his hazel eyes had little flecks of gold in them that sparkled in the sunlight.

Unfortunately, Peter Weston had taught her that looks could be crushingly deceiving. And despite all of Ridge's good points, Marianne couldn't get past the aggravation he'd already caused her. Coming in late with a crazy flying display that nearly gave her a heart attack was just the start. Then there was the mock RSVP that caused her to waste money on a catered meal for his plane. *No doubt about it,* Marianne decided as the ceremony wound down.

Ridge Collins was walking trouble.

While Matt and Caty sealed their vows with a long kiss, everyone stood to applaud and cheer. Caty turned, and Marianne dutifully handed over her bouquet of pink-and-white roses.

"We've been friends forever, and now we're sisters!" Caty exclaimed, embracing first Marianne and then Lisa. "How cool is that?"

"Very cool," Lisa agreed as the two of them exchanged a very unladylike high five.

"Excuse me." Matt stepped in and tapped his new bride on the shoulder.

When he motioned down the aisle, she laughed and took his arm to make their ceremonial first walk as man and wife. After they rounded the corner of the house, he swept her up in a hug, giving her a kiss that seemed to go on forever.

When she realized she was spying on them, Marianne turned away to give them some privacy.

And straight into the best man.

Ridge offered her his arm. Still agitated by her conflicting impressions of him, she quickly invented an excuse for not taking it. "The kids are saving you a seat, so go ahead and sit down. I'll join you after I see if the caterers need anything."

"Sure. Let me know if I can help."

People were settling in for their meal, and she watched the new Mr. and Mrs. Sawyer make their way through the garden, stopping at each table to talk with their guests. Tears stung her eyes, and she took a deep breath to calm her churning emotions. She was happy for them. Thrilled, actually. She wouldn't let her baffling reaction to the best man or memories of her own failed marriage ruin this day for two people she loved so much.

She'd had her chance, and it hadn't worked out. That didn't mean Matt and Caty were destined for heartache.

Please, God, she prayed silently. *Bless them with a long, happy life together.*

Late that afternoon, Matt and Caty said goodbye to their last wedding guest. Marianne expected them to be as exhausted as she was, but they seemed to have caught a second wind. After hugs and thank-you's for everyone, they climbed into Matt's enormous blue pickup. Streamers and cans flying along behind them, they drove around the circular drive, waving out the windows before heading toward the main road in a cloud of dust.

The silence they left behind was deafening.

The family just stood there, watching the truck go down the highway until it disappeared over a hill. For fifteen years, they'd waited and prayed for Matt to come back from wherever his wanderlust had taken him. Their father's unexpected death had finally brought him home, and Caty's love had kept him there.

But now he was gone. Oh, he'd still be in Harland, but he'd be living with Caty in their new house. The family would see him while he was working at the farm, maybe for a meal now and then. But his heart belonged to Caty, and he wanted to be with her—should be with her. The rest of them would have to adjust, but Marianne knew it wouldn't be easy.

"They'll be back," she said out loud, as much to herself as to anyone else. "Two weeks isn't that long."

"It's forever," Emily moaned, her chin trembling while she stared down at her wilting bouquet.

Marianne swept her up for a comforting embrace. "They'll be back before you know it. Everything will be just fine."

"You're set if I go, right?" Lisa asked. "I'm beat."

"The servers are handling the cleanup," Marianne replied, giving her a quick hug. "Thanks for all your help."

"No problem. Ridge, it was nice to meet you." Shaking his hand, she added her usual dazzling smile. "If you get hungry, I work at Ruthy's Place on Main Street. We'll fix you up with some honest-to-goodness home cooking."

"Do I look like I need it?" he asked.

"Every man does," she retorted.

"Ruthy, as in Ruth Benton, the amazing chef who catered the wedding?"

"The very same. You come in, I'll set you up." Flashing him another smile, she sauntered over to her car and gracefully slid into the driver's seat.

After her sister's flirtatious exit, Marianne snuck a look at Ridge, fully expecting to find him watching Lisa go. Pretty and carefree, Lisa was a starry-eyed dreamer who adored people, men especially. Males of all ages were drawn to her sunny personality. They just couldn't help it.

Not this one, though. To Marianne's amazement, he was engrossed in a discussion with Kyle about the faulty motor on his remote control helicopter. Something about servos was all she understood.

"I'm done, too," John announced, stooping to kiss Marianne's cheek. "You sure do throw a great wedding."

As he strolled down the lane toward the converted carriage house he lived in, she shook her head. A ratty pair of sneakers had replaced his good shoes, and he'd shed his jacket and tie sometime during the day.

Because their mother had died when he was only five, Marianne had mothered him since childhood, and he still counted on her to look after him. Later, she'd find his missing clothes and get them cleaned, but this time she'd give him the bill. He was almost thirty, and it was time for him to start doing more on his own.

Right now, she had company. Still holding Emily, she turned to Ridge. "Come on inside. I'll fix us a snack."

"I had enough from that buffet to last me a week," he replied, patting his stomach. "I'd love some more of that lemonade, though."

They headed up the back porch steps with the kids, and he stepped in front of her to pull open the screen door. Thanking him, she set Emily down in the kitchen.

"Emily, where are your pretty new shoes?" she asked as Kyle snagged some chocolate chip cookies from the jar in the middle of the table. He thought he was being sneaky, but he'd been so good all day, she let it go.

Innocent blue eyes looked up at her. "In the pond."

"Why?"

"They were hurting my feet."

While she was counting to ten, Marianne noticed the red streak on her daughter's dress. "What's this?"

Emily glanced down like the spill was news to her. "Punch."

She really didn't have the energy for this, Marianne thought, swallowing a sigh that would only make matters worse. "Go take it off and bring it down for me. If we soak it, we might be able to get the stain out."

The suggestion earned her a world-class pout, and Emily wrapped her arms protectively around herself. "No. I like my dress."

"I do, too. I want to get it clean so you can wear it again."

Now those sweet eyes glared up at her defiantly. "No."

It had been a long day for all of them, and Marianne had finally reached the end of her patience. "Emily Rose—"

"Hey, Emmy," Kyle interrupted, "I'm goin' swimming. Wanna come?"

How he'd inhaled those cookies so fast was beyond Marianne. But his idea made Emily forget the argument, and she nodded enthusiastically.

"Let's go put our suits on," he said. "I'll race you!"

Squealing, she took off with him trailing close behind her. Typical Kyle, he let her win the race upstairs. Two bedroom doors slammed shut, and a couple minutes later Marianne heard the front screen door squeak open. She looked out the window to see Emily tearing across the lawn toward the pond. Another set of footsteps pounded down the stairs, and Kyle reappeared in the kitchen, grinning as he handed over the stained dress.

"Here you go, Mom. Good luck."

"Wait for me before you hit the water!"

He waved without turning around, and she felt silly for saying it. As responsible as most adults, Kyle knew the rules, and he followed them to the letter. Her little man, Marianne thought proudly. Every day she thanked God for sending him to her.

Emily was hollering his name, and he yelled for her to run out to the barn to spring his dog. They came back into view with Tucker barking excitedly as he ran circles around them and begged for attention from Kyle, then Emily, then Kyle again.

"Whew," Ridge commented as he dropped into a chair at the table. "Is it always like that around here?"

Marianne smiled as she opened the fridge and

poured them both some lemonade. "With the wedding, they're a little more wound up than usual. Now that school's out, things should calm down a little. I'm a teacher, so I'll be off with them all summer. Lots of their friends end up here, which makes it fun."

He chuckled. "I'll bet."

Of course, she wasn't entirely certain she still had a job. Her teaching position was a one-year contract filling in for Kathy Walsh, who'd been on leave recovering from back surgery. Kathy would return in the fall, and Marianne was waiting anxiously to find out if Harland Elementary had a spot for her. If not, she had to find one somewhere else. With budget cuts and declining enrollment throughout the area, that wouldn't be easy.

Pushing the worry from her mind, she set their glasses on the table and plopped down across from Ridge. Slipping off her grass-stained pink satin shoes, she crossed her feet on another chair and took a long swallow of the first thing she'd actually tasted all day. "Mmm."

"Your kids are fantastic, Marianne," Ridge said. "Emily could charm a statue, and Kyle's something else."

Like the proud mother she was, she smiled at the praise. "Yeah, he is. I don't know what Emily and I would do without him."

Emily's dress was still sitting on the counter

where Kyle had thrown it. Marianne had just gotten comfortable, but she knew if she didn't get it soaking, the punch stain would never come out. Reluctantly, she stood and crossed the kitchen to get the stain remover from its handy place on the ledge over the sink. With two active kids, she used it frequently.

"Just so you know," Ridge continued, "Matt said I could keep Betsy here and use his bike if I need it."

Rubbing the remover into the delicate fabric, she chuckled at her big brother's forgetfulness. "Of course he did."

"I know she's not your usual houseguest. I can rent some hangar space at the airstrip if that works better."

"It's not a problem. We have plenty of room."

While she rinsed the fabric in cold water, Marianne tried to keep her expression neutral. A grin slowly spread across Ridge's tanned face, and she knew she hadn't quite managed it.

"You don't like chaos, do you?"

"Not really," she admitted.

"Funny how Matt never mentioned that."

"It must have slipped his mind." Like telling her his best man would drive her completely bonkers the minute she met him.

Chuckling again, Ridge shook his head. "Caty's really gotten to him, hasn't she?"

The way he phrased it, it sounded romantic and sweet, even a little exciting. But Marianne couldn't muster more than a faint hum of agreement as she applied more stain remover to Emily's dress.

"You're not happy about them getting married?" Ridge asked, clearly—and understandably—perplexed.

"I'm very happy."

"But?"

Hoping to steer him away from the uncomfortable subject, she decided to keep it vague. Setting the dress in the sink, she turned to face him while she wiped her hands on a towel. "Things don't always work out the way we want them to."

"That's true. I'm divorced myself."

He said it matter-of-factly, as if it weren't a big deal. Divorce was against everything she believed in, a broken promise to God. Five years later, she still hadn't come to terms with her failed marriage.

"You look upset," Ridge sympathized.

Completely forgetting her manners, she shot back, "And you don't. Why is that?"

He shrugged. "Sometimes things don't work out. My wife wanted a different life, and I let her go find it. We're both happier now," he added, as if that made everything okay.

Appalled by his casual attitude, Marianne glared at him. "The vows are 'until death do us part,' not 'until things don't work out.'"

Ridge studied her for a few seconds, compassion etching his features. "I'm guessing your ex is the one who left. Could you have stopped him?"

"Yes," she retorted immediately, even though she knew it wasn't true. She'd come home to find Peter's wedding ring on the counter wrapped around a note that read *I want a divorce—Peter.*

Ridge slowly shook his head. "You don't really believe that, do you?"

His perceptiveness was more than a little unnerving. She'd never met a man so adept at reading people, and she didn't know what to think.

Eager to end their pointless conversation, she said, "I don't mean to seem rude, but the kids are waiting for me."

"I wouldn't mind a dunk myself. Mind if I come along?"

"Not at all."

Cocking his head, he grinned at her. "You're just being polite, aren't you?"

Caught in the half lie, she smiled. Ridge's open, forthright manner made her want to strangle him one minute and laugh the next. "I was, but now I mean it. You're welcome to come with me," she added as she headed out the side door.

When they saw her on the side steps, Kyle and Emily raced down the dock and dove into the pond. His feathery tail going a mile a minute,

Tucker anxiously waited on the bank, watching the kids. Once he was satisfied they were ready, the black Lab barreled down the dock like a furry jet and launched himself into the water.

The cool grass felt heavenly on her tired feet, and Marianne walked down the dock and settled on the end to dangle them in the water. Ridge stretched out beside her, but gave her plenty of space. After their far-too-personal chat, she appreciated the gesture.

"Watch me, Mommy!" Emily called out, dog-paddling toward the opposite bank for all she was worth.

"Great job," Marianne said. "All that practice is really paying off."

"I want Kyle to toss me, but he won't."

"Next year, Emmy," he promised. "You hafta be seven for that."

And able to swim back to the surface, Marianne added silently. Still, she was grateful to Kyle for handling his little sister so deftly. Emily adored him, and she wanted to do what he did. Sometimes they had to hold her back because she refused to accept that she couldn't keep up with him. Marianne always got an argument or, at the very least, a first-class pout. Kyle managed to slide bad news past his little sister with a diplomatic flair that would come in handy at the United Nations.

After a while, Tucker climbed from the pond and shook out his fur. Ridge greeted him, and the dog flopped onto his back in a less-than-subtle pose. Laughing, Ridge rubbed the lab's wet belly.

Since he hadn't spoken to her, Marianne decided it was up to her to start a more pleasant discussion. She decided to go with something less emotional than weddings and divorces. "So, tell me about your date."

He laughed at her joke. "Betsy's a 1941 Stearman. Grandpa towed it home with most of the parts missing or in boxes. We spent the better part of five years putting her back together."

"You and your granddad built that airplane?"

They both turned at the sound of Kyle's voice. Elbows braced on the dock, his hazel eyes were round with admiration. He'd been following Ridge around like a puppy all day, and Ridge was surprised to find he liked the attention. It's not that he didn't like kids, he just never gave them much thought. This bright, curious boy had definitely impressed him.

"That's so cool," Kyle said with a wide-open grin.

"Yeah, it was."

Unlike the dark images of his wreck of a father, Ridge had great memories of time spent with his grandparents. He and his mother's father were more alike than not, and they had a blast working together. Everything he needed to know about being a real man, Ridge had learned from Grandpa.

"It sounds like flying is your family business," Marianne said.

Since he didn't have many warm, fuzzy stories to tell, talk of family always put him on shaky ground. As usual, Ridge focused on the positives. "After World War One, my great-great-grandfather flew all around the Midwest as a barnstormer. They put on some great shows back then, aerial tricks and wing-walking, all kinds of stunts."

"It's in your blood, then," she commented. "Like this farm's in ours."

"I guess so." Emily had paddled over to join them, and Ridge smiled from one kid to the other. "I'll bet this is a great place to grow up."

"The best," Kyle agreed as the kids climbed the ladder and sat on the towels spread on the dock beside their mother. "Where do you live?"

Ridge thought for a second, trying to simplify his complicated history. "I'm from Colorado, as I said earlier, but I've lived all over. California, Montana, Texas. I spent most of last year in Alaska."

"Alaska?" Kyle echoed. "What did you do there?"

"I was a bush pilot. Took people out on wilderness tours, delivered supplies to the way-out villages, stuff like that."

"Why do you move so much?" Emily asked.

No one had ever asked him that quite so directly. Maybe, like Marianne, adults figured it was too personal a question. "I like to explore different places, I guess."

"I like it here," Kyle said simply. "Someday this place will be ours. Right, Mom?"

"Definitely," she assured him with a proud smile.

Kyle nudged his sister's shoulder. "We're gonna take real good care of it, aren't we, Emmy?"

Emily's vivid blue eyes glowed with brother worship, and she nodded somberly. She probably had no idea what she was agreeing to, but it was about the cutest thing Ridge had ever seen.

"How old are you again?" Ridge teased Kyle.

"Ten and a quarter."

Impressed by the very precise way he gave his age, Ridge recognized the serious demeanor from his own childhood. He knew firsthand that when dads were out of the picture, little boys grew up fast. Sadly, his own experience had taught him there were worse things than an absent father.

Pushing those memories aside, he smiled at Emily. "How 'bout you, sweetness?"

"Oooh, I like that name," she cooed. "I never had a special name before."

"I'm glad you like it."

Score one for the new guy, Ridge thought with a grin. Welcoming as the Sawyers had been, he still felt like an outsider looking in on the close circle of their family. Because he moved around so much, he was used to that. He couldn't for the life of him figure out why it was bothering him all of a sudden.

Pulling her Cinderella towel around her shoulders, Emily said, "I'm six. I was born a long way away from here."

"Really? Where?"

Emily glanced up at her mother, who nodded. "Chicago. Daddy didn't want us, so me and Mommy and Kyle came back here to be with Granddad." She frowned. "He's with Gramma in heaven now."

Marianne smoothed her hair with a comforting hand, and Kyle put an arm around Emily's shoulders for a quick squeeze. The way she'd skimmed over her father's rejection of them just about stopped Ridge's heart. While he'd already guessed that Marianne's ex had left them, it hadn't occurred to him just how much that would have affected her children.

What kind of man pushed away a beautiful

woman and fantastic kids like these? Emily's revelation made the Westons' family situation painfully clear to Ridge, but he reminded himself that it was none of his business.

"Your uncle Matt told me all about your granddad," he said gently. "He sounds like a great guy. I wish I could've met him."

What would his life have been like if he'd had a generous, loving father like Ethan Sawyer? Grandpa did his best to fill the void, but all his life Ridge had known he was missing out on something. Since there was no remedy for his very flawed past, he did what he always did when thoughts like that popped up. He pushed them aside and focused on the here and now.

"We miss him all the time," Emily continued sadly. "We loved him a lot."

"I love my grandpa, too. He taught me everything I know."

"Like what?" Kyle asked.

"Like how to pick off a runner at first base or throw a good, tight spiral with a football. How to fix an engine. How to fly," he added with a fond smile. "All the important stuff."

He almost expected Kyle to ask about his father. He braced himself for it, but the question never came. Young as he was, Kyle struck him as an old soul who understood more than any ten-year-old should. Ridge wondered if somehow the kid sensed that they shared father trouble and had decided to give him a break.

"I hate to do this, but we need to get you two into some dry clothes." Marianne stood and held her arms out for them. For Ridge, she had a gracious smile. "Are you hungry yet?"

Remembering the manners Mom had pounded into him all his life, Ridge got to his feet. While he appreciated Marianne's hospitality, he sensed that after the long day she'd had, she wouldn't mind some time alone. "Actually, I need to do a few things with Betsy. Thanks, though."

"The offer stands. My kitchen's always open."

As the three of them walked toward the house, their voices trailed back to him, punctuated by the kids' laughter. Despite her gracious behavior, anyone could see that Marianne was exhausted. All day, she'd been a real trouper, managing one thing after another with a lovely smile he suspected had taken her years to perfect.

Did women practice that kind of look? Ridge wondered as he strolled toward Betsy's makeshift runway. Came in handy when they decided it was time to cut you loose but didn't want to mortally wound you. He had no trouble imagining the very proper Marianne Weston dismissing a guy that way.

A rose with thorns, he mused as he pulled his tool kit from Betsy's storage compartment. Grabbing what he needed, he began degreasing the rebuilt engine he'd installed last month. Full of original parts and expertly machined reproductions, it had cost him a small fortune. But, with care, it would last for years. Like anyone else, Betsy was at her best when she got the attention she needed.

Speaking of which, Tucker trotted over and sat in front of Ridge, shamelessly begging for some love. Ridge hunkered down and fluffed his damp ears. "You're quite the character. Dogs don't usually take to me so quickly."

The Lab cocked his head with a curious look, and Ridge laughed. "You don't know you're a dog, do you?"

In response, Tucker yipped and spun a quick circle before taking off for the woods. As Ridge watched him go, he took a minute to admire the Sawyer homestead. Over two thousand acres, Matt had informed him proudly when he'd asked about it. The land had been in the family since the mid-1800s, and every square inch was obviously worked with care, even the fallow field he'd used as a landing strip.

A well-worn dirt path wound past John's cottage and up to the main house. There it joined up with a wide driveway that split two rows of fence and trees on its way out to the road. Ridge could tell from the structure of the walls that the original farmhouse had been expanded over the decades as the Sawyers needed more space. Each outer door led to a generous porch, but the front one was the showstopper.

Draped in ivy, trellises ran top to bottom to support every color of climbing rose he could imagine. Thanks to his grandmother, he knew enough about gardens to recognize that those flowers weren't trucked in as wedding decorations. They grew there year-round, tended as meticulously as the inside of the immaculate house.

That was Marianne's doing, he knew without being told. She struck him as organized and disciplined, caring for everyone and everything around her. Instinctively, he knew she was someone who took charge and made sure things got done. Like him in some ways—vastly different in others.

Based on the few words they'd exchanged since he arrived, she didn't seem the least bit interested in him. That was actually a relief, Ridge thought with a sigh. Life had taught him that he was the kind of person who withered when he stayed in one place too long. He'd tried it more than once and failed every time, managing to hurt himself and the people he cared about most.

As soon as he finished the dusting contracts Matt had thrown his way, he and Betsy would be back in the air where they belonged.

Chapter Two

Sunday morning, Marianne woke up bright and early. The house was silent, and outside her window she could hear the birds enjoying the misty sunshine. The kids were still sleeping after the busy wedding day, and she opted to leave them be until breakfast was ready.

Today would be much calmer than yesterday, and she decided to take advantage of the quiet. The chair she'd rocked Emily in as a baby still sat next to the window, and a breeze came through to flutter the sheer curtains around it. It was an inviting sight, so she sat down and picked up her devotional book from the side table. The next lesson started with a line from Corinthians.

Let all that you do be done in love.

Quotes followed from various people—some pastors, other regular folks with inspiring stories to tell. Marianne read through them but nothing resonated with her. While she appreciated the general idea of doing even small things with a loving heart, for some reason she couldn't focus on the words long enough for them to make a solid impression.

Despite her best efforts, her mind kept wandering back to Ridge's unusual arrival. In her memory she saw him climbing down from his plane, turning to face her for the first time. Despite her best efforts to be merely polite, she had to be honest with herself.

The man fascinated her.

Cocky and self-assured, he seemed to assume that people would like him just as he was. She'd had that kind of confidence once. Back before her marriage had disintegrated and stripped away everything she'd thought was so solid.

Seeing Ridge's eyes sparkle while he told them about his ancestors' exciting adventures explained why he enjoyed flying so recklessly. Maybe it was in his blood, maybe he was imitating men he admired, but their courageous example had helped make him who he was. More than that, she knew he was proud of those men. Despite his gypsy-like lifestyle, Ridge's family history meant something to him.

Now that she owned the home Daniel Sawyer had built so many generations ago, Marianne's connection to her own family's past was stronger than ever. She could certainly appreciate that in someone else.

The clock on her night table told her it was time to get moving. On her way to the bathroom, she glanced into each of the kids' rooms to find them sound asleep. After her shower, she put on her new blue dress and quickly pulled her hair into a twist. She added Grandma Sawyer's beautiful pearl choker and earrings but left her feet bare. They were still sore from yesterday, and she decided there was plenty of time to wedge them into a pair of heels later on.

When she was ready, Marianne tiptoed downstairs to sneak in a little more peace and quiet before things went haywire. The programmed coffeemaker was already brewing, so she went to the fridge to pull out the egg-and-sausage casserole she'd made for this morning. Setting the oven, she slid the pan in and walked out to get the newspaper.

The headlines never seemed to change all that much, she mused as she poured coffee into a mug proclaiming her *Best Mom Ever.* She was in the middle of reading a book review when Ridge stumbled through the back door. He looked like he hadn't slept a wink.

"Coffee," he croaked. "Please."

Trying to be polite, she did her best not to smile, but he looked so pathetic she couldn't help herself. To make up for it, she got up to fill a mug for him. "Rough night?"

Dropping into a chair, he answered with a huge yawn. "John snores like a freight train. Around three, I gave up and went to get my headphones out of Betsy so I could get some sleep." He swallowed two sips in rapid succession. "Excellent coffee."

"Thank you."

Men liked it strong, so she always added an extra scoop. What she didn't tell him was she blended French vanilla in with the regular. If he found out, she knew he'd never drink another cup.

When Ridge seemed a little more coherent, she asked, "So, what do you think of Caty?"

"She's great."

The gold in his hazel eyes twinkled mischievously, telling her that was all she was getting. He wasn't going to come right out and admit that Matt had told him nothing about the woman who was now his wife.

"You never met her before yesterday?" Marianne tried again.

"Nope, but Matt loves her. That's good enough for me."

In her experience, men didn't normally take

emotions at face value that way. They needed proof, numbers—things like that. "You have a lot of faith in him."

"Yeah, I do." Curiosity lit his eyes, and he leaned toward her. "Can I ask you something?"

"Sure." His direct gaze made her want to squirm, and she fiddled with the handle on her mug to avoid it.

"Matt and John get along, don't they?"

"Very well. Why?" She met his gaze.

"So why didn't he ask his little brother to be his best man?"

"John didn't want to do it," she explained. "He said it would cramp his style at the reception."

"Right." Ridge dragged the word out in a sarcastic tone.

This man was really starting to irritate her. One minute he was a total charmer, and the next he was a cynic. "What are you saying?"

"I think Matt's trying to set us up."

"That's crazy," she protested. "Why would he do that?"

"You know how it is when a friend gets married. They want everybody to be as happy as they are."

"Matt wouldn't do that."

Ridge cocked one disbelieving brow and, far-fetched as the idea seemed, she had to admit he could be right. Matt had changed a lot since Caty came into his life. It was possible he wanted to introduce his old friend to his little sister and had used the wedding as an excuse to get them together. But why Ridge Collins? she moaned silently. She was rooted in Harland with her children, and this free-spirited pilot flew wherever the wind took him, doing whatever he pleased. They had absolutely nothing in common.

Hoping to change the subject, she sipped her coffee. "Why didn't you come in for supper last night?"

"I didn't wanna impose on you and the kids."

She sighed. Apparently, she hadn't been as gracious yesterday as she'd intended. Setting her coffee down, she swallowed her pride. "I'm sorry about coming down on you about your divorce. I had no right to judge you that way."

"Don't worry about it. You didn't say anything I haven't thought a million times in the last two years."

He was being so nice about it, she felt even worse. But he seemed content with putting it behind them, so she decided to follow his lead. "We've got eggs and sausage for breakfast. Would you like some?"

"Thanks, but no. I've got work to do, and I'd best get started."

"We all go to church on Sunday mornings,"

she commented lightly. "You could come along if you want."

"I appreciate the invite, but it's not really my thing." Draining his mug, he stood and smiled down at her. "You make fantastic coffee."

Marianne tried very hard not to criticize people, but his lack of interest in attending Sunday service annoyed her. As their guest, it would only be polite for him to accompany them to church. But if she'd learned anything about Ridge in the short time she'd known him, it was that he did exactly what suited him, no matter what other people might think. In her mind, it wasn't one of his better qualities.

As he headed for the door, she asked, "When will you be back?"

"Later."

"For lunch?"

A heavy cloud seemed to descend over his usually lighthearted demeanor, and he frowned. "I'll be back when I'm done."

"I'm not trying to rope you into anything. I just want to know how many people I have to feed."

"That's nice of you, but I take care of myself."

With that, he all but fled the kitchen and pounded down the back steps. Completely exasperated, Marianne grabbed his empty cup and rinsed it before putting it in the dishwasher. Still fuming, she started pulling dishes from the cupboard.

"I take care of myself," she mimicked as John came through the back door. She didn't know how he did it, but he always managed to show up just when the food was ready.

"Lemme guess." He grinned at her. "Ridge."

"I was trying to be considerate, and he brushed me off."

"He's not used to having folks waiting on him for meals and stuff." Very predictably, John defended him. "He kind of does his own thing."

"That's obvious," she retorted as Lisa came through the door.

"What's obvious?" Lisa asked, picking up the plates from the counter to set around the table.

"Ridge does his own thing," John explained with a grin. "It drives the queen crazy."

"I noticed that yesterday," Lisa commented with a grin of her own. "Quite a few sparks there."

"No." Marianne pointed a stern finger at her starry-eyed little sister. "No sparks. Irritation and aggravation, but no sparks."

"Still irritated and aggravated." John dragged the sports section loose, which fanned the rest of the neatly folded paper across the table.

"I'll say," Lisa agreed. "She couldn't care less

about any of the guys around here. What's so special about Ridge?"

"Not a thing," Marianne shot back.

"Sure," Lisa scoffed, adding a laugh that grated on Marianne's nerves.

Fortunately, the kids came trotting down the stairs, and Marianne announced, "I think I'll make waffles to go with that casserole. Who wants some?"

"Me." Without looking up, John raised his hand while he and Kyle scanned last night's baseball scores.

"I'll help you, Mommy," Emily offered eagerly, skipping into the pantry to get her ruffly white apron from its hook.

The familiar routine helped soothe her frayed nerves, and Marianne settled in to enjoy breakfast with her family.

"Such a beautiful wedding," the Sunday school teacher complimented Marianne when she dropped Kyle and Emily off for their class. "It couldn't have been more perfect, could it?"

Marianne agreed with her, as she had with everyone who'd said the exact same thing to her this morning. "Everything worked out just the way we wanted."

After saying goodbye to the kids, Marianne

went upstairs to join John and Lisa. While she was near the back of the church, Pastor Charles hurried over and intercepted her.

"Marianne, I want to thank you again for including Penny and me in your celebration yesterday. We really enjoyed ourselves."

"Oh, I'm glad," she replied with a genuine smile. The jovial man in the gray suit and paisley bow tie had married her parents and baptized them all. He held a special place in the Sawyers' hearts. "That was the plan."

"If you don't mind…" Leaning in, he whispered, "My wife wants the recipe for your double-berry pie. I promised her I'd ask."

Marianne laughed. "It's one of our favorites, too. I'll email it to her later today."

"Bless you." Beaming, he patted his ample stomach. "Not that I need any more of it, mind you, but I sure do enjoy it."

After thanking her again, he turned and headed for the pulpit. The white church wasn't large, and this morning it was standing-room only. Fortunately, John and Lisa had saved Marianne a seat. Looking around, she greeted everyone nearby with a smile. After starting her morning wrangling with Ridge, seeing all these familiar faces gave her a calm, contented feeling.

As she sat down, Lisa grinned. "We're the talk of the town."

"Better watch it, Mare," John teased. "You'll end up as the Harland wedding planner."

"Not a chance. One was more than enough."

"What about us?" Lisa asked, puffing out her lower lip in a slightly more grown-up version of Emily's famous pout. "We're gonna need your help, too."

If her flirtatious baby sister ever settled on one man, Marianne would be amazed. If John someday found the girl who could lasso his roving heart, she'd be stunned. Then again, she'd never imagined Matt settling down, either. God had stepped in on that one, for sure, so it was entirely possible He'd do it again.

Buoyed by the thought, she smiled. "Okay. Two more, but that's it."

"Till Kyle and Emily," Lisa said.

"Please." Marianne groaned, only half joking. "Don't marry my babies off just yet. I'm not ready."

Laughing, Lisa put an arm around her shoulders and hugged her. "Deal."

The affectionate gesture felt especially good this morning. Marianne was still unsettled, and she wasn't sure why. She kept telling herself it was the prospect of adjusting to life at the farm without Matt, but she knew that wasn't quite right. Accustomed to reasoning things through, she wasn't adept at listening to her instincts. But she was smart enough to know they were trying to tell her something.

She just couldn't figure out what it was.

The organist began with the opening chords of "How Great Thou Art," and they all stood to sing. It was one of her favorite hymns, the first she'd learned after "Jesus Loves Me." The comforting verses always made her think of her parents. Despite her mother's tragic illness, her parents' unshakable faith in God and each other had shown her what true love was all about.

Now that they were both gone, she found herself turning to God even more often, relying on His strength in addition to her own. She had to be strong, to make sure Kyle and Emily wouldn't miss the father who'd abandoned them and never looked back.

As she had since she was a little girl, she stared at the stained-glass window over the altar, admiring the vibrant colors of Jesus and the animals surrounding Him. To her, that picture represented His infinite wisdom and endless compassion for every creature on earth. The hymn came to an end, and she felt her tangled thoughts starting to unravel.

Despite her still-baffling mood and the uncertainty about her job, a genuine peace settled over Marianne's heart, and tears of gratitude stung her eyes. She knew God saw every struggling sparrow, but it was nice to be reminded that He saw her, too.

They were all sitting down to lunch when the distant buzz of Ridge's plane interrupted their conversation.

"Can we go out and watch him land?" Kyle asked, already halfway out of his chair.

A hundred percent male, he loved anything that went fast: Matt's Harley, John's Triumph convertible, now Ridge's plane. She had to accept it, Marianne reminded herself. Her little boy was growing up, and she loved him too much to hold him back.

Hoping her sudden funk didn't show, she smiled. "Let's all go."

With an excited whoop, he took off like a shot with Emily on his heels and the rest of them trailing behind. The kids ran down the lane until Marianne warned them to stop so they wouldn't be too close to Betsy's landing strip.

Goodness, she berated herself. Now she was calling the plane by name. Clearly, Ridge's nuttiness was contagious.

After a minute or two, she noticed that Ridge wasn't coming in to land. He was skimming low over their planted cornfields, spraying dust that would keep bugs and rot from destroying the crops as they grew. At the end of each long row, the plane looked like it couldn't possibly pull up soon enough to avoid crashing into the woods. Yet somehow, Betsy made it every time.

"That's so awesome!" Kyle exclaimed, pointing into the distance so Emily could follow the runs. "Ridge must be the best pilot in the world."

Marianne didn't know much about flying, but she admired his skill. He made the little plane dive like a hawk, then rise gracefully back into the air to circle around for another pass. Even though she had no desire to take a ride, she couldn't help wondering what the sprawling Sawyer Farm looked like from the air.

Ridge must have spotted them all standing there, because the plane banked and came toward the house. Waving from the open cockpit, he rocked the wings back and forth. Screaming and waving back, the kids jumped up and down with delight. She saw him grin before whipping into a full barrel roll that took him over their heads and perilously close to the tops of the trees.

"He's going to crash in the woodlot," she predicted in a tight voice.

"Nah," John assured her with a grin. "Ridge knows what he's doing."

Marianne wasn't convinced of that. But she was certain that he'd once again turned her very carefully planned schedule upside down. "He was supposed to dust here tomorrow."

"Does it really matter?" John asked.

"I close the windows when they dust," she explained, "and make sure the kids aren't here while all that pesticide is floating around."

"We really liked it, Mommy," Emily added, looking up at her brother. "Didn't we, Kyle?"

"Yeah," he breathed, eyes fixed on the plane as it looped around and came to rest on its makeshift runway. "Ridge is so lucky, being able to do that."

Even though she'd never admit it to anyone, Marianne couldn't agree more. With her own confidence in tatters, she admired the courage Ridge showed in the air and on the ground. Fearless and confident, he seemed to assume that things would work out for the best. His fun-loving personality showed when he flipped the plane like it was a kite and began his descent.

She was grateful for the life she and her children enjoyed, settled in this safe, cozy place. But she couldn't help wondering how it felt to have the wind rushing past you while you flew through the clouds, free as a bird.

To avoid damaging the field any more than he had to, Ridge brought Betsy to a gentle stop in the same marks he'd already made. As he shut the engine down, he looked out to see a line of people headed his way, the kids running in front. He was seldom in one place more than a few weeks, so people didn't usually make such a fuss over him. Between the wedding and today, he'd gotten more attention than he had in the last six months. For a habitual wanderer like him, it was kind of fun.

"That was awesome!" Kyle said approvingly with a huge grin. "Did you see us waving?"

"Sure did." Ridge smiled at him and then Emily. "I wasn't putting on a show for the corn, y'know."

While John complimented him, Ridge was only half listening. He was more curious about the expression on Marianne's face. He was used to women being impressed with him, or at least with his flying. The problem was, she didn't look impressed.

She looked annoyed.

For the life of him, he couldn't imagine why. Then she filled in the blanks for him.

"I thought you were dusting tomorrow."

Her clipped tone told him she was irritated with the change in plans, and he waited a beat to make sure he sounded professional. "The forecast is for rain tomorrow and Tuesday. I moved up my jobs to make sure they got done, so the spray wouldn't get washed off before it had a chance to soak in and do its work."

The glacial temperature of her eyes warmed a little, and she nodded. "Well, that makes sense."

When the others headed back inside, she turned and followed them. As he fell in step beside her, Ridge took a shot at what might be bothering her.

"Don't worry about paying me," he said. "I'll be around."

"This farm is a business, and we pay people what we owe them when it's due."

She refused to look at him, and he sighed in resignation. "I didn't mean to insult you. It's just that Matt and I are friends, and I don't want to make things tough on you. Financially," he added, to be sure they were clear on that point. In the short time he'd known her, Marianne had struck him as someone who liked to dot her *i*'s and cross her *t*'s.

She didn't respond to that, and he figured it was best to keep quiet. Then she surprised him.

Glancing over at him, she said, "Thank you for doing those tricks for the kids. It was nice of you."

I'm a nice guy was on the tip of his tongue, but he thought better of it. He hated to sound pathetic, like he was trying to convince her of what most people got right off the bat.

So he settled for, "I'm glad they liked it."

He wondered if she'd enjoyed the show, too, but figured it would be lame to ask.

"I also want to thank you for helping John clean up the tables and chairs last night," she added. "He said it took half as long as he thought it would."

"No problem. Just pitching in where I could."

She didn't say anything else as Ridge followed her up the front porch steps and through the double doors. From the large entryway, one arch led into the living room and another to an office.

In direct contrast to the neat but lived-in look of the rest of the house, this room was ruthlessly tidy. Every surface was clear of papers, which he assumed were filed in the row of cabinets along the far wall. The walls were a fresh cream color, with family pictures from many generations scattered all around.

One on the desk caught his eye, and he picked it up for a closer look. Anybody with half a brain could tell it was the Sawyers. All of them. Ridge had never met Matt's parents, but he smiled at the happy family sharing a picnic somewhere. The little girl hanging over their father's shoulder looked a lot like Emily, and he pointed to the grinning face.

"Is this you?"

Marianne glanced over, and a sad smile dimmed her features. "Yes. That was taken just before Mom got sick."

Her last good memory of her mother, Ridge realized with a frown. No wonder the little frame held the place of honor on her desk. Very carefully, he set it down and wandered over to the windows. One looked out over the front garden while the other framed the pond, making it seem like a landscape painting. Except for the sleek laptop and printer on the large desk, the scarred antique furniture appeared to have been here since the house was built.

"Great spot." He strolled over to admire her view of the pond. "Must be nice working in here."

"It is," she replied as she sat down and opened a program on her computer. While her fingers clicked on the keys, she asked, "I know your name, but what's your address?"

"My mom's will work." Still focused on the pond, he started reciting it.

"Wait a minute," Marianne interrupted. "You don't have an address?"

Facing her, he shrugged. "Not really. Most folks get me through my cell or email."

"Where do you live when you're not working?"

"I'm always working," he said, then grinned. "Or never working, depending on how you look at it. Grandpa always says if you love what you do, you never work a day in your life. That kinda sums me up, so he got it engraved on a brass plate and mounted it on Betsy's dash the day of our first flight. I don't think he invented the saying, but— What?"

She was shaking her head, looking truly appalled. Ridge was getting that gross specimen feeling again.

After several uncomfortable seconds, she said, "I'm still trying to understand how a man your age with a successful business doesn't have an address."

"Not everybody likes being rooted in one place."

He didn't know why he felt compelled to defend his lifestyle to her, but he couldn't help it. He wasn't one to second-guess his choices, but for some reason this pretty, soft-spoken woman was beginning to mess with his confidence.

"Meaning you think I do?"

From the way she hurled the words at him, Ridge knew that despite his best efforts, he'd managed to insult her.

"I assume so, with your kids and everything," he said, trying to soothe whatever nerve he'd struck. "You grew up here, and you're still here. That's nice."

"For me," she filled in, still challenging him. "But not for you."

"Settling doesn't work for me."

"You think I've settled?" She jumped to her feet like he'd attacked her. "You don't know the first thing about me."

"I didn't mean it like that."

He tried to explain that he'd meant *settling down*

wasn't right for him because, despite searching from coast to coast, he'd never found a place where he really wanted to stay. But he could tell she wasn't hearing him anymore.

Marianne ripped his check from the printer and signed it in a furious scrawl. After shoving it into his chest, she pivoted on her heel and stormed out.

Chapter Three

Marianne's unforgivable outburst with Ridge followed her like a thundercloud all day. She'd been short-tempered and mean, which was very unlike her. Hard as she tried, she just couldn't shake her dark mood. She knew perfectly well that he hadn't intended to put her down or in any way suggest that her life was less fulfilling than his.

Unfortunately, knowing that didn't help lift her spirits. After a marathon session of laundry and housework to work off some of her frustration, she exhausted herself to the point where she felt more normal. Not entirely, but close enough to be better company.

Later that afternoon feeling contrite for being so prickly, she let Kyle talk her into playing Monopoly. Most days, the long, involved game didn't suit her very well because it gobbled up so much of her precious spare time. But her kids loved it, even though she wasn't sure Emily totally understood the rules. As a teacher, Marianne recognized that the game was good practice for adding numbers and counting spaces. For the kids, the fact that they always beat her was a definite bonus, and she went along because it made them so happy.

Today, it was the perfect way to apologize for her behavior without having to invent an explanation for it.

"I'll buy it," Emily announced when she landed on her fourth railroad. She didn't have enough money, but Kyle was the banker and he gave her the deed card and some "change" that would keep her in the game.

Kyle loved to win, and Marianne was impressed by the generosity he'd shown his sister. She reached over to ruffle his hair, but he pulled away and she settled for an approving smile. When the screen door creaked open, she glanced up to find John coming in for his usual Sunday afternoon leftovers raid.

"There's more in the fridge on the side porch," Marianne said as she tossed the dice for her next move. Counting out the spaces, she groaned when her impoverished terrier landed in front of Kyle's hotel.

"Welcome to the Boardwalk," he crowed, holding out his hand. "Two thousand, please."

"Aw, man," John sympathized. "How much have you got?"

"Fourteen dollars." She surrendered it and her piece to Kyle, who promptly buried the dog under the hotel that had bankrupted her.

"Nice," John chided him as he plunked himself down on the bench next to Kyle. "Nothing like having a heartless zillionaire in the family."

The comment rattled Marianne, and she prayed her son hadn't inherited his father's ruthless streak. If he had, she'd have her hands full reining it in. There was no way she'd just stand by and let him follow in Peter's greedy footsteps.

"I still have some money, Uncle John." Emily waved two fifties in the air. "And I'm gonna pass Go on my next turn."

"Good for you, darlin'." Crossing his arms on the table, he nudged Marianne's elbow. "How're you doin'?"

Puzzled by the question, she leaned back and saw uncharacteristic concern in his eyes. "Fine. Why?"

"You seemed off earlier today. Lisa was worried."

"But not you?" Marianne asked, although she knew the answer. He might lack polish, but her carefree younger brother had a tremendous heart.

"Maybe a little. So what's my answer?"

"Just tired is all," she said. Even to her own ears, she sounded unconvincing.

"Wouldn't have anything to do with tomorrow's date, would it?"

As soon as he said it, she knew what had been eating at her all weekend. She hadn't consciously realized it, but he was right.

Eleven years ago tomorrow, she'd married Peter.

Tears threatened, and she swallowed hard to keep them under control so she wouldn't upset the kids. After so long, she was dismayed to discover that those memories hadn't faded. They were lurking in the shadows, waiting for an opportunity to burst free and hurt her all over again.

"I guess," she managed, forcing the words around the sudden lump in her throat. "I hadn't thought of it until now."

He gave her a smile of encouragement. "Lisa's working this afternoon. I'll stay with the kids if you wanna go talk to her."

Marianne prided herself on being strong and competent. She hated asking for help, even when she probably needed it. Although she was no psychiatrist, she assumed it stemmed from becoming the Sawyers' mother hen when she was only seven.

The kids' laughter got her attention, and she looked over at them. Tucker was paws-up on the table, nosing through Kyle's enormous pile of money.

"I'm fine," she repeated.

"Come on," John scoffed, tilting his head with a doubtful look. "This is me you're talking to."

Lisa was such a great sounding board, Marianne was tempted to take him up on his offer. But she seldom left the kids with anyone, even family. It felt wrong somehow. To avoid insulting him, she hedged. "I don't know. The diner might be busy."

"On a gorgeous day like this? Everybody's off fishing or having a picnic somewhere. That place is probably a ghost town. She'll be glad for the company. And when was the last time you went out on your own?"

"Christmas," she shot back.

"Sure, to shop for presents for all of us."

Again with the tilted head. He was reminding her more of Tucker by the second, but she had to admit that John's suggestion made sense. Times like these, she really wished she could talk to her father. Even if he didn't have a solution, Dad had always listened, reminding her that she didn't have to manage everything on her own.

"Kids, I have some errands to run in town. Will you keep an eye on Uncle John for me?"

They agreed enthusiastically, and he grinned. "That reminds me, can you stop by Gerber's and pick me up some socks?"

"What happened to all your socks?"

"Tucker." He nudged the Lab's belly with his bare foot. "He goes nuts over 'em."

"You shouldn't let him in your house."

"That'd be no fun at all." Reaching into one of the cargo pockets on his shorts, he pulled out a very thin nylon wallet and opened it. After rummaging through, he looked up and gave her one of his gotta-love-me grins. "I'll pay you back."

"If you and the kids stay out of trouble while I'm gone, we'll call it even."

"Done. I'll handle supper, so you don't have to come back till after that."

"Yay! Uncle John's making supper!" Emily approved, clapping her hands. "Can we have chocolate cake?"

John let out a groan. "Are you *trying* to get me in trouble?"

"As if you needed any help with that," Marianne teased.

"We'll do something your mom would be okay with."

He flashed Marianne an angelic smile she wasn't buying for a second. But after they shook on their deal, she went into the pantry to get her purse from its hook. The newspaper on top of the recycle bin caught her eye. The book reviews were showing, and she tore the page out. Gerber's sold everything, including the latest bestsellers. Instead of wallowing in memories of her failed marriage, maybe she just needed some time to herself to read more than a few pages of a book. A piece of one of Ruthy's blue-ribbon desserts wouldn't hurt, either.

It wasn't like her to be so impulsive, and the prospect of breaking loose for a while definitely appealed to her. Feeling better already, she kissed the top of Emily's head, fist-bumped Kyle and headed out the door.

"Ruthy, this isn't peach cobbler," Ridge insisted as the first forkful practically melted in his mouth. "It's a dream."

"Well, thank you." The petite woman behind the counter refilled his coffee. "There's plenty more if you want it."

"Count me in."

Before going down to the other end of the counter, she gave him a warm, motherly smile that crinkled the corners of her cornflower-blue eyes. Judging by the traces of gray in her light brown hair, he pegged her somewhere between fifty and seventy. But she struck him as one of those people who didn't really age because they simply refused to get old. His grandfather was like that, and Ridge had every intention of following his example.

While he enjoyed his pie, Ridge admired the diner's charming country style. He ate most of his meals out, so he'd been in plenty of restaurants, but none of them compared to this. With pale-green-checked curtains and well-used tables and chairs, it had the look of a place the locals genuinely enjoyed. The collection of knickknacks on high shelves along each wall caught his attention, and he examined each piece with curiosity. He was wondering about the life-size black rooster when the bell over the door chimed, and he glanced down to see who was coming in.

Marianne Weston.

He spun his stool around so she wouldn't see him, and barely fought off the urge to bury his face in his hands like a two-year-old. His last conversation with her had turned into a losing battle for him, and only a masochist would invite another one. Ridge suspected that she felt exactly the same way.

To his great relief, Lisa popped her head over the swinging kitchen door and winked at him. She came out to hug her sister, turning her away from the counter and aiming her toward a booth in the back. Ridge appreciated her running interference for him, but he decided it was best not to tempt fate.

As Ruthy came his way, he handed her enough to pay for his dessert with a generous tip. "That was fantastic, but I think I'll take a rain check on the extra piece."

As she slid the money into the pocket of her ruffled apron, she didn't say anything. When she looked up, she gave him a knowing smile. "Ridge, are you up for a little advice? It's on the house."

"Sure."

"Sometimes the toughest nuts have the sweetest hearts. Do you know what I mean?"

This kindhearted stranger had nailed his problem dead-on, and he couldn't hold back a grin. "Yeah, I do. But I've tried all different kinds of nuts, and I won't be having any more. They don't seem to agree with me."

"They're not all the same. Some are even worth the trouble it takes to crack them open."

"Mind if I join you?"

Marking her place with her napkin, Marianne glanced up to find Ridge standing by her table. She'd noticed him at the counter when she came in, but he was talking to Ruthy so she hadn't interrupted. Seeing him now made her wonder if God was telling her—none too gently—to explain her erratic behavior to the poor, unsuspecting man who'd borne the brunt of her temper tantrum.

"Not a bit." She put her book away and smiled

as he sat down. "I'm glad you came over. I owe you an apology."

He gave her a puzzled frown. "For what?"

After a sip of water, Marianne filled him in on her John-inspired epiphany.

"Yeah." Ridge nodded. "That makes sense."

Not to her, she thought, but it was nice of him to try to make her feel better about it. "Things have been so crazy with the end of school and the wedding and all, I never even thought about it."

"You didn't really forget, though. Your subconscious knew, and it was making you miserable."

Surprised by his insight, Marianne shook her head. "That's what Lisa said when I told her about it just now. You two must listen to the same radio shrinks."

Completely unfazed, he grinned back. "Some of what they say makes sense. If folks paid more attention to their hearts and less to the space between their ears, they'd be a lot happier."

"Is that your secret?"

"You betcha. Fretting about stuff you can't control doesn't change a thing. It just sucks the life out of you."

Marianne wished she could share his perspective. She envied his easygoing disposition, the way he seemed to ignore things that drove her completely bananas. Then again, his full sum of obligations was his business, an old plane and a beat-up duffel bag. It was easy to be even-keeled when your boat didn't get rocked on a daily basis.

"If I tell you something you won't like," Ridge began, "do you promise not to shoot the messenger?"

Talking to Lisa and now him had drained most of her tension away, and Marianne was feeling more generous. "Sure. Go ahead."

"Your family never liked your ex."

"The boys didn't like Peter," Marianne corrected him. "They told me every chance they got. It wouldn't surprise me if they even said it to his face."

"Matt told me Lisa and your dad agreed with them. None of them liked the way he treated you. Matt said it was like the guy thought you were just something pretty to show off."

"Why didn't Dad and Lisa say something?"

Ridge shrugged. "Maybe they figured you saw something in him they didn't, and they loved you, so they decided to keep quiet."

Marianne's heart sank, and she sighed. "It looks like I'm the only fool in the family."

"Not a fool," he amended with a sympathetic smile. "In love. Sometimes people change, or it turns out they're not who we thought they were."

Marianne's thoughts drifted to the rocky start

she and Ridge had gotten off to. Matt had very few friends, but he'd chosen the restless pilot as his best man. That meant he trusted Ridge, a big deal for her reserved brother. Maybe there was more to their guest than met the eye.

"I should get going," Ridge said, standing up from the table. "Betsy's probably refueled by now, and I should get back to work."

Giving her a much-needed smile of encouragement, he left Marianne alone with her book.

After several chapters and two decadent pieces of pie, Marianne finally felt ready to go home. When she got there, she found John in the kitchen, whipping up his specialty—scrambled eggs and grilled-cheese sandwiches. Glancing at the clock, she realized she'd been gone almost four hours. When mom guilt started in, she firmly pushed it back. She'd needed a break, and she'd taken it, she told herself firmly. Her children had fun with their uncle while she enjoyed some alone time.

Everybody won, and she was no longer a contender for the Wicked Witch award. It was all good.

The kids were at the table cleaning up the pieces from a game of Sorry. Several boxes were stacked on the counter, telling her John had managed to keep them busy while she was gone.

Setting her shopping bags on the counter, Marianne kissed the top of Emily's head and patted Kyle's shoulder. "It looks like you had a good time."

"We sure did," Kyle said. "Ridge was kinda wandering around, so I invited him in for some lemonade and he ended up staying a while. He really likes your lemonade."

"It's the vanilla." Standing on tiptoe, she kissed John's cheek. Very quietly she said, "Thanks for the break."

"No problem." Balancing a sandwich on his spatula, he asked, "Want one?"

"Sure, thanks." She sat down at the table with the kids. "Did you let Uncle John win any of these games?"

"Nah, that's cheating," Kyle informed her. "Ridge said we had to beat him fair and square."

"You don't get anywhere in life if people just hand things to you," Emily added in a very serious voice. "You have to learn it."

"Earn it," Kyle corrected her with a grin. "It means you worked for something and deserve to have it."

"Ohhh." She nodded. "That's important."

"It sure is." Marianne smiled her thanks as John set a plate in front of her. Ridge's lesson on deserving to win impressed her. No doubt, he'd gotten it from the grandfather he so obviously admired.

"Just so you know," John said casually, "I invited Ridge to the Fourth of July picnic. He wasn't planning on staying that long, but I thought it'd be nice for him to see Matt and Caty when they get back."

"Fourth of July!" Emily crowed, clapping her hands. "Can we get a bounce house, Mommy? And a waterslide like last year?"

"More fireworks," Kyle added while he chewed. Marianne glared at his poor manners, and he swallowed. "Sorry. Could we please get more fireworks this year? That way Granddad can see them from heaven."

Those words just about broke her heart. It would be their first Fourth of July celebration without her father, and she shared Kyle's feelings. Emily's excitement faded and she looked down at her half-eaten sandwich. "I miss Granddad."

"We all do, darlin'," John assured her with a fond smile. "But he's still around the farm every day, keeping an eye on us."

She lifted her head, and her eyes rounded in amazement. "He is?"

"Sure. The folks we love are never really gone," he explained. "As long as we remember them, they're always here."

Marianne was stunned, to put it mildly. She loved John, but she'd never heard him talk that way. She knew that their dad's unexpected death had affected them all, but she hadn't realized how much it had changed her carefree little brother.

Right now, though, he pinned her with a knowing look. "You forgot about the picnic, didn't you?"

Even though she was thoroughly embarrassed, Marianne couldn't hem and haw with her children listening. So she did her best to laugh it off. "With the wedding and everything, I'm ashamed to say I did. We'll fix that, though." Crossing the kitchen, she picked up a piece of chalk and started a list on the blackboard. "Bounce house. Waterslide. Fireworks. What else?"

"A pony!" Emily chirped.

"I can handle that," John said. "The Perkins have a nice little Shetland they use at the fairs. I'll trade them some hay for an afternoon with Dopey."

"Dopey?" Emily scowled. "That's a mean thing to name a pony."

"I guess it's their grandson's favorite dwarf. He's three."

"I hope when he's older, he picks better names," she said with a disdainful sniff.

John grinned at her. "I'm sure he will."

"Maybe Ridge could give people rides in his plane," Kyle suggested hopefully. "That would be really cool."

"Ridge is our guest," Marianne reminded him. "I don't think he wants to work on the Fourth."

The door creaked open, and the man himself stepped into the kitchen. "What's this about working on the Fourth?"

She relayed Kyle's idea, and she could see excitement sparkling in Ridge's eyes. He spun a chair around and sat down. "I'd be happy to give rides. What else have you got planned?"

While the kids filled him in, Marianne watched him closely. He showed the same interest in Emily's fanciful ideas as he did in Kyle's more practical ones. Ridge wasn't childish, but he had a childlike enthusiasm she grudgingly envied. Even though he was in his mid-thirties like Matt, Ridge had managed to keep the little boy in him alive all these years. That shouldn't have held any appeal for a thirty-year-old mother of two, but for some reason it did.

"Sounds fantastic," he approved with a genuine smile. "How can I help?"

"You any good with a lawn mower?" John asked.

"It's been a while, but I'm sure I can handle it. That reminds me." Suddenly, he was serious. "If you need an extra pair of hands while Matt's gone, let me know. I hate staying here and not helping out."

"Well, now, I don't get too many offers like

that." John rocked his chair on its back legs just because he knew it drove Marianne crazy. "You sure you know what you're getting into?"

"The dusting comes first, but afternoons I only have some aerial tours scheduled. I could give you a few hours when they're done."

"I just might take you up on that."

While John filled him in on what they'd be doing around the farm, Marianne was only half-listening. She'd thought Ridge considered himself their guest, but apparently he felt obliged to earn his keep. As Matt's friend, he could stay as long as he wanted, tending to his contract work while John kept their shorthanded farm running as smoothly as he could. That Ridge would even think to lend a hand certainly impressed her.

Maybe, she mused, he really was one of the good guys.

As Ridge had predicted, the rain started early Monday morning, accented by thunder and lightning that kept Tucker cowering under the kitchen table, whimpering like a puppy. Marianne and the kids were sorting through their school papers, deciding which were important enough to keep. Emily's pile wasn't much smaller than when they'd started, but most of Kyle's was heaped in the recycle bin. Typical, Marianne thought with a little smile.

While she was mixing up some fresh lemonade to go with their oatmeal cookies, the phone rang.

"Sawyer Farm," she answered, tucking the handset between her chin and shoulder while she stirred ice into the pitcher.

"Marianne, this is Donna Harvey. Principal Franks was wondering if you have some time to meet with him around one today."

Marianne's heart shot into her throat, and the spoon kept spinning in the pitcher when she let it go to grip the phone properly. This was the call she'd been waiting for, the one that would set her plans for the foreseeable future.

Harland Elementary was either offering her a full-time permanent teaching position, or they were letting her go. Traditional to the core, Alan Franks was the type of man to deal with both tasks in person.

Marianne took a deep breath before answering. "That works into my schedule perfectly, Donna. Please tell Alan I'll be there at one."

As she pressed the off button, Marianne quickly rearranged her chores to accommodate this very important meeting. After pouring each of the kids some lemonade, she did her best to sound casual.

"Kyle, I've got a meeting at school at one

o'clock. Can you go find Uncle John and let him know I need him to hang out with you two while I'm gone?"

With the driving rain, she knew John was enjoying a rare day off. She hated to interrupt that, but she couldn't take the kids with her to a meeting with the school principal. Donna wouldn't mind having them wait in the office lobby, but Marianne felt it would be unprofessional to ask for that kind of favor.

"Ridge is in the barn," Kyle said as he bolted for the door. "I'll ask him."

"I don't—" The rest of her protest was lost in the slamming of the screen door, and she looked at Emily with a little grin. "He really likes Ridge, doesn't he?"

Swallowing a mouthful of cookie, Emily gave her a sweet smile. "So do I, Mommy. He's awesome."

That was Kyle's word, and hearing her daughter use it made Marianne chuckle. Sitting at the table, she asked, "What do you like so much about him?"

"He calls me 'sweetness,' which is very pretty. Mostly, he listens to me when I'm talking. I really like that."

Funny, Marianne thought while she nibbled on a broken cookie. She liked that about him, too. Through the screen, she watched as Kyle and

Ridge paused outside the barn and evened up their feet. Growing up with two very competitive brothers, she recognized a race in the making.

She heard Kyle shout, "Three, two, one, go!" and the two of them ran toward the house. Ridge beat him to the porch easily enough, then stumbled and groaned loudly as Kyle flew past him and up the steps.

"Klutz," Kyle taunted his muddy opponent with a huge grin. "I told you it was slippery."

"Whatever," he grumbled.

When he looked at Marianne, there was an unmistakable twinkle in his eyes that told her he'd tripped on purpose. *So much for not letting kids win,* she thought with a smile. "I didn't mean for Kyle to pull you away from what you were doing."

"Just puttering. What's up?"

Considering the shaky nature of their new friendship, she hesitated to ask him for a favor like this. But since her only other option was to take the kids with her, she forged ahead. "I was hoping you and John could watch the kids for me while I go to school for a meeting."

"Mommy's going to be a real teacher," Emily informed him proudly.

Ridge looked to Marianne for clarification, and she explained. "I've been a sub this year, but I'm hoping for a permanent position. The principal wants to talk to me about it."

Ridge gave her a sympathetic look. "Or?"

He'd read her insecurity so quickly, it took Marianne by surprise. Keenly aware that her kids were listening, she did her best to disguise her very real fear. "I'll find another one."

"If you teach half as well as you do everything else, any school would be lucky to have you."

The conviction in his voice told her he was dead serious. Stunned by his response, she stammered, "Thank you."

Glancing at the clock, he pulled out a chair and helped himself to a couple of cookies. "I'd imagine you've got some things to do before you go. I'll find John and then make sure the kids have something besides these for lunch," he added before taking a huge bite.

She appreciated his understanding that she'd prefer her brother be there with the kids. While Ridge seemed responsible enough, she'd only known him a couple of days.

"Can we watch a movie?" Emily asked. When Marianne hummed, her daughter gave her a dimpled smile. "*May* we watch a movie?"

"Sure," Ridge agreed easily. "You can each pick one."

"I want to pick first," she announced.

"That's not fair," Kyle protested. "I'm the oldest, so I should go first."

"Aw, man," Ridge groaned as he got to his feet. Digging something out of the pocket of his jeans, he said, "You can flip for it."

Intrigued, Kyle craned his neck to see the coin in Ridge's hand. "That's cool. What is it?"

"It's a Walking Liberty dollar," he answered, holding it on his palm for them all to see. The well-worn silver piece shone in the light, and he smiled. "Grandpa gave it to me when I was a kid, for good luck."

"Does it work?" Emily asked, eyes bright with curiosity.

"Well, I've had a pretty good life," Ridge replied. "I'd say it doesn't not work."

Apparently satisfied with the luckiness of the silver dollar, Emily said, "I want heads."

"That'd be the lady, then." He flipped the coin and caught it on the back of his hand. When he pulled his other hand away, the woman glittered up at them. "Sorry, dude. Emily picks first."

"Great," he grumbled. *"Princesses."*

"Nuh-uh." With her button nose in the air, she said, *"Lion King."*

Marianne knew her very boyish son would never admit it, but that was still one of his favorite movies. With a long-suffering sigh, he said, "Okay."

"That's settled, then," Ridge commented as he put the coin away. To Marianne, he said, "You should probably go get ready."

"Yes, I should. Thanks again."

"No problem. And Marianne?"

Pausing at the foot of the stairs, she looked back.

Dragging his hands back through his soaking-wet hair, he grinned. "You might wanna take an umbrella."

"So," Donna said while she typed, "how was the wedding?"

"Fun," Marianne replied, trying not to stare at the principal's closed door. "It was a lot of work, but it was worth it to see Matt and Caty so happy."

Donna hit the enter key and turned to her with a bright smile. "Knowing you, it was like one of those bride's magazines."

Being a perfectionist, nothing ever suited her completely, but Marianne appreciated the praise. "Now we're looking forward to summer vacation. How about you?"

"Water park, county fair, lots of dirt-track races and demolition derbies." Donna ticked each of them off on her fingers with a good-natured grin. "Maybe someday I'll have a girl and we can do the spa thing while Tim hangs out with the boys."

Marianne felt a little envious of Donna's good

fortune. Peter had never voluntarily done anything with the kids, but she kept dragging him to the zoo and the playground so they'd have some family time. In the end, it was a colossal waste of time. It would have been so nice—

"—this guy Tim works with."

Marianne was jerked back to the present. "What?"

"He's a corporate lawyer at Tim's firm, never married, no kids. He's been focused on his career, and he's really successful. Now he's looking for someone to share all his toys with. We've gotten together a few times, and he seems really great. So, naturally, I thought of you."

"Why?" Marianne blurted out before she realized it would sound incredibly rude. "I mean, I appreciate the thought, but I'm not really interested in dating right now."

Donna gave her a you-can't-fool-me look. "How long have you been single?"

"Not nearly long enough to even consider getting back into all that." Marianne made a face. "Besides, I don't have time."

"Right."

Feeling even more self-conscious than she had when she got there, Marianne fished around in her purse like she was searching for something.

In reality, she just wanted to end the pointless argument with someone who clearly meant well.

Something fluttered out, and she picked it up off the floor. When she laughed, Donna tilted her head and smiled. "What is it?"

"One of my students gave me this on the last day of school." Marianne showed her a hand-lettered invitation to supper. On the front was a crayon picture of his house, but no address. "He said his father needs someone to go places with. He told me his sisters keep trying, but they get it wrong."

"Really?" Donna said, her smile growing. "Did he say why?"

"According to him, girls don't know what guys like."

The friendly receptionist laughed out loud. "That is so true. And very sweet of him to step in to try to help his father find a girl. Are you going?"

"I didn't have the heart to turn him down in person." Marianne refolded the drawing and slid it into the side pocket of her purse. "I told him I'd think it over and let him know."

"Why would you turn him down?" Donna asked. "His dad could be a great guy."

Marianne swallowed a groan. Folks seemed to have no problem telling her what—and who—she needed to be happy. She appreciated their concern, but she wished they'd all just leave her be.

Her wrenching divorce had stripped her of everything except her children and her dignity, which had taken a real beating. She wasn't keen on wading back into those waters anytime soon.

"I won't mention it again." Donna finally relented, hands in the air like she was surrendering. "But I think it's interesting that a first-grader can see what's missing in your life and you can't."

"I have Kyle and Emily, and a big farm to help run. I've got more than enough already."

"You really believe that?"

"Yes." That wasn't entirely true, but Marianne did her best to sound convincing. She'd done that a lot in the last few years, waiting for her natural confidence to return. She had no clue how long that would take, but until it happened she'd just have to fake it.

Shaking her head, Donna sighed. "Suit yourself, I guess. You won't mind if I say a few prayers for you, though, will you?"

"Of course not. I'll take all the prayers I can get."

The intercom buzzed, and Donna picked up the phone. After hanging up, she gave Marianne an encouraging smile.

"Then I'll start right now. Alan's on his way out."

As she stood and smoothed her skirt, Marianne

realized that her hands were shaking. She took a deep breath and felt reasonably calm when the principal opened his door and greeted her with a smile.

"Thanks for coming in, Marianne," he said, offering his hand. "I know it was short notice."

Hoping to sound unconcerned, she said, "It wasn't a problem at all."

Still smiling, he led her to his office and motioned for her to sit in one of the comfortable chairs opposite his desk. After closing the door, he strolled over and sat down behind his desk.

"I'd imagine you're a little anxious about this, so I'll get right to the point." Another smile. "You've been a wonderful addition to the Harland teaching staff, and we'd like to offer you a permanent position."

Marianne's heart soared, and she swallowed down the excited yelp that was threatening to burst free. Very professionally, she simply said, "Thank you so much. I accept."

Alan cautioned her with a raised index finger. "One thing first. We have high standards for our teachers, and you'd have to meet them."

"Of course. What do I need?" At this point, she'd stand on her head and eat a bug if the school board told her to.

"Your master's."

Now her heart sank. While she could figure out a way to pay for classes, she didn't have the time to shuttle back and forth to the nearest campus an hour away in Charlotte. Worse, her life was built around her children, and she couldn't imagine spending all her free time in class and studying.

The problem was, she knew that in order to get a full-time position anywhere, she'd probably need that degree.

"I understand your hesitation," the principal continued. "You're an excellent teacher, so we'd waive the practicum requirement. But we can't make an exception for you on the degree."

"I wouldn't want you to," she replied, meaning every word. "High standards mean our students get the best possible education. That's what all parents want."

Approval lit his eyes, and he nodded. "I was hoping you'd say something like that. Do you want some time to think it over?"

"No, but I do have a question." When he motioned for her to go on, she asked, "Which grade level is available?"

"First, the same class you taught this year." He chuckled. "After all that time off recuperating, Kathy decided to retire rather than come back. She and her husband took an RV trip to the Grand Canyon and enjoyed it so much, they're going to

become professional gypsies. Her words," he clarified with a grin.

She'd be teaching her favorite age group, Marianne thought with a grin of her own. In the school
her children attended, so they could still ride with
her if they wanted to. While the prospect of going
back to college was daunting, she'd figure something out.

She knew this was God's way of adjusting her
course to get her back on track, and she wasn't
about to second-guess Him.

"Going part-time, it could take me a while," she
pointed out. "Is that a problem?"

"As long as you're enrolled in classes and pro-
vide us with your grades, we'll be happy."

As much as she wanted to just dive in, she hesitated. "This affects my family, too. I should talk
to them first."

"Not a problem. Let me know what you decide."
Alan stood and extended his hand. "You're a talented, inspiring teacher, Marianne. We'd be lucky
to have you here."

His parting words echoed what Ridge had said
earlier, and as she left his office, she took that as
a good sign. When she got home, the kitchen was
empty, while the TV in the living room flickered.
John and Ridge were stretched out side by side on
the floor, their heads propped against the couch.

The kids were at either end of the sofa, listening to Simba and Nala sing about falling in love. Tucker lay on top of them in his usual movie-watching spot.

"Hey, there," Ridge said, sitting up to look at her. "How'd it go?"

"They offered me the job." They all started cheering, and she raised a calming hand. "The problem is, I have to get my master's degree. That's going to take a lot of money and time."

"We'll all help out," Kyle promised. "I can help Emmy with her homework while you do yours."

"I can make dinner sometimes, Mommy," Emily added in a very grown-up voice. "I know how to do PBJs, and Uncle John can teach me how to make grilled-cheese sandwiches."

"Sure thing, darlin'," he agreed with a bright grin that shifted to Marianne. "Sounds like you've got it covered."

"Except for the money," she corrected him. "It's bound to be expensive."

"You can get on a payment plan with the college," Ridge told her. "And student loans have real low interest rates."

"How do you know that?" she asked.

"Mom's getting her bachelor's so she can teach special ed. She's been an aide for years and decided to go all in."

"I guess that could work," Marianne allowed, buoyed by their quick acceptance. No one had voiced a single concern, questioning how her new schedule would affect them. "Now I just have to figure out how to manage my own classes while I'm teaching."

"Mom's taking some of hers online. I'll bet UNC does the same thing."

Ridge was just full of great ideas, she thought with a smile. "I'll check that out. It would be a good way to start."

"I have one question," he said. When she nodded, he went on. "Will this make you happy?"

Without hesitation, she nodded. "Very."

"Then go for it. You deserve to be happy."

Tucker barked in agreement, and Marianne laughed as she walked toward her office. "Okay, then. I'll get the ball rolling."

"Take your time," John told her. "Emily can make supper."

Chapter Four

"They're here!"

Pulling away from Marianne, Emily ran to meet Matt's truck in the driveway. He stepped out and swung her up for a hug, tossing her in the air while she laughed. "Welcome home, Uncle Matt! We have a pony named Dopey."

Setting her down, he grinned. "Just for the day, I hope."

She nodded eagerly. "Uncle John borrowed him. He's really cute, Aunt Caty," she added as the newest Sawyer joined them. "Come see."

"I'll be right over," Caty promised with a hug for her and then Marianne. "First I need to see if your mom needs some help."

"Everything's under control," Marianne told her. "Go ahead."

Emily tugged Caty toward the awning John had

set up for their adorable guest, and Matt draped an arm around Marianne's shoulders. "Miss me?"

"About as much as you missed us," she teased, smiling as he kissed her cheek. "Thanks for the phone calls and postcards."

He gave her a shameless male grin. "We were busy."

John strolled over and welcomed him home, then said, "We need ice."

"We do not," she protested. "I have coolers full of it."

A mischievous grin spread across his tanned face, and she smacked him. "Don't do that to me. I can make sure you have to eat your own lousy cooking."

The buzz of Ridge's plane circling for a landing interrupted his smart comeback, and Matt shaded his eyes to follow the biplane to the ground. "How's he doing?"

"Fine," Marianne replied. "Why?"

Matt shrugged as they headed toward the picnic tables ringing the pond. "No reason. He's not usually in one place this long is all."

"You didn't tell me he was such a good mechanic," John said. "Whatever breaks, he can fix it. And he's not a bad hand with a cultivator, either."

Her brothers drifted toward the grills while John

caught Matt up on what had happened at the farm during his honeymoon. Marianne took a seat at an empty table, scanning the spread-out crowd for anything needing her attention. It was one of those perfect summer days that would keep everyone outside until dark, which fit their fireworks plans to a T.

Her entire first grade class was there, along with their families. Kyle and Emily's classmates and friends were enjoying kickball and playing inner-tube tag in the pond. There was a—more or less—friendly game of horseshoes going on over in the pit John had made. Observing it all from a safe distance, the members of the Harland Ladies League commented to each other while their husbands tried not to listen. Their president, Priscilla Fairman, actually pulled out one of those expensive new electronic tablets and started taking notes.

When she began snapping pictures, Marianne smiled and shook her head. The Sawyers' Fourth of July bash would be all over the social media sites by morning.

Sipping her sweet tea, she checked on the kids in the bounce house, then counted heads on the waterslide to make sure they weren't overloading the equipment. She'd put Kyle in charge there, and it looked like he had things under control. After a few trips around the front yard, Dopey had lost his charm for everyone but Emily. Lisa had graciously set up a little picnic for them near the awning so Emily could enjoy the pony for as long as he stayed.

Of course, that left Marianne with nothing to do. She wasn't used to that, but she decided to enjoy it while it lasted. Tucker loped up behind her and stuck his nose under her hand for some love.

"Hey, you." While she petted him, she straightened the new Stars and Stripes bandanna Ridge had bought for him to wear today. "Are you having fun?"

"Yeah, it's awesome."

Ridge's voice answered from behind her, and she laughed as he took the open space on the bench beside her. "For a second there, I thought he'd learned how to talk."

"He just might one of these days." Ridge added one of his easygoing grins. "Smartest dog I ever met, that's for sure."

"When we came back here, Dad had this puppy waiting." She patted his head, thinking back to that day. "It made things a little easier for Kyle."

"How 'bout you?" When she didn't answer right away, he frowned. "Sorry. Sometimes stupid things just pop out of my mouth."

A few days ago, she'd have bristled at the highly

personal question and refused to answer. But in the time Ridge had been with them, she'd learned he wasn't rude, just straightforward.

"That's okay. It's a reasonable question." She added a smile to let him know she wasn't angry. "After Peter left, I was so lost I didn't know what to do. Thankfully we had a place to go. Dad wasn't thrilled with the divorce, but he told me over and over how happy he was to have us here. When people asked, he'd say he thoroughly enjoyed my cooking and having clean clothes just show up in his drawers."

Chuckling, Ridge swallowed some tea. "It must've been tough to give up your independence, though."

"At first, but I never really liked Chicago." Looking around, she smiled at the laughter and animated conversations going on. "Harland is a much better place for the kids. We had a fifth-floor condo in the city, and the park was up the street, so it was always a big production to take them there. Here, they can play outside and I don't have to worry about them running down the road to a friend's house."

"Yeah, the country's great for kids."

She heard envy in his voice, and she wondered where he'd grown up. "What about you? Did your family move around a lot?"

He gave her a puzzled frown. "Why would you think that?"

"Your business takes you all over, and you said you don't like being in one place. It would make sense if your family was that way."

"Yeah, that would make sense."

She waited for him to continue, but suddenly he was looking everywhere but at her. She hadn't known him long, but she'd gotten accustomed to the way he focused on whoever he was talking to. He was so up-front with people, it seemed odd that he'd be avoiding her now. This was the first decent conversation they'd had, so she didn't feel right digging for details.

But she couldn't help wondering what on earth he was hiding.

Marianne came through the door with an armful of groceries, not surprised to find John in the kitchen. It was close to lunchtime, and a Sawyer boy never missed a meal. That was how they got so tall, she thought with a smile.

"Is Ridge coming in, too?" she asked as they headed out to help the kids unload her minivan.

"As soon as he wrestles a new belt onto that old baler."

That meant nothing to her, and she laughed. "I'll take that as yes, he's having lunch with us."

"Yup. By the way, Charlie Simmons called. One of his assistant coaches broke his leg yesterday."

"Oh, no," she groaned. "What happened?"

"Waterskiing. Tried to impress his kids by doing a flip."

"Idiot." They set down their bags, and the impact of the man's injury hit her like a ton of bricks. "Can he coach football with a broken leg?"

"Not a chance. Charlie's freaking out, hunting for somebody to take his place."

"Minicamp's next week, Mom." Scowling, Kyle piled on more gloomy news. "If we don't have enough coaches, we'll have to cancel camp and we'll be behind all the other teams when the season starts."

"What would you like me to do?" she asked while she emptied bags into the refrigerator. "I don't know the first thing about coaching football."

Kyle turned to John with a hopeful expression. "Could you do it?"

John's hangdog look said it all. "With all I've got going on here, I can't. I could help out once in a while, but I can't be at every practice, and that's what you need."

"Maybe Uncle Matt could do it."

"Same problem." John sat down at the table, looking even more dejected. "We planted an extra two hundred acres of hay this year, and it's keeping us busy."

"Everybody works, Kyle," Marianne pointed out gently. "Camp isn't so bad, but it's not easy to free up ten hours a week for the whole season."

Kyle fell silent, and she wished there was some kind of mom magic she could do to fix this. He was obviously making an attempt to take things in stride, but she knew he was upset. He just didn't want to make John feel any worse than he already did.

"Coach Simmons said if we don't have enough coaches when the season starts August first," her son said quietly, "the league won't let us play."

She'd forgotten that rule, which elevated the problem to full crisis status. The Wildcats had never dealt with it before, so it hadn't been an issue. Until now. While she was mentally running through a very short list of potential replacements, a voice floated in from behind her.

"What does it take to be an assistant coach?"

Turning, she found Ridge in the doorway with Tucker. As he opened the screen door, she couldn't believe she hadn't heard him come up the back porch. Then again, Tucker's heavy panting had probably drowned out his footsteps. Padding toward his bowl, the dog slurped up half the water and flopped down on the cool tile floor. He rolled onto his side, his tongue hanging out like he didn't have the strength to go one more step.

"You take a class online," John answered. "Then you get together with the other coaches and work out your plays, get to know the kids, help run the camp. At first it's Saturday mornings, then ten hours a week when the season starts. Once they're in school, you cut back to six hours of practice so the kids don't drop. And then there are the games on Sundays."

"Sounds workable." Ridge turned a chair around and sat down. He traded looks across the table with Kyle. "Your team any good?"

"We came in second last year. This year we're taking the championship."

Marianne admired his determination, but he was her son so she was slightly biased. She was pleased when Ridge grinned his approval. "What position do you play?"

"Wide receiver on offense, linebacker on defense," Kyle said. "I had eight sacks last year."

"Awesome. I was a quarterback. All-state three years running."

"Both my uncles went all-state four years." Kyle trumped him with a proud grin. "Uncle John was top wide receiver his senior year, and Uncle Matt won best linebacker in the whole conference. Twice."

"He's the man, all right," Ridge agreed without hesitation. "I played some sectional games against Harland, and he killed me every time."

"I thought you and Matt just met a few years ago," Marianne said, wondering again about his penchant for moving around.

"Officially. During high school, I lived near here, but Matt and I only knew each other on the field." He gave her a wry grin. "It's hard to recognize a guy in a helmet who hits you so hard you can't see straight."

"That's my big brother." John chuckled. "They called him the Wrecker."

"What did they call you?" Kyle asked him.

"Hands." He held them up, palms out, as proof. "Good for basketball, too. You guys played before my time," he said to Ridge, "but I remember watching those games. They were great."

"Good bunch of guys on those teams," Ridge agreed, turning to Marianne. "I'd hate to see Kyle and his buddies miss out on that. The sport's about a lot more than football."

She knew that. Team dynamics and working hard to reach a goal helped foster responsibility. Although she'd never played any sports herself, she was an avid armchair athlete. Whether it was baseball or soccer, she enjoyed the strategy and opportunity for everyone to contribute, whatever their size or ability. In junior football, the coaches were required to use all their players, which meant everyone bencfited from being part of the team.

The coach's injury left them short of time to find a replacement, so substituting Ridge seemed like the perfect solution. But she had one major reservation about this man who'd literally dropped from the sky and into their lives.

"Ridge, may I talk to you outside a minute?"

"Sure."

John didn't even bother trying to conceal a grin, and she could almost hear Kyle's eyes clunking as they rolled around in his head. She had to give Ridge credit, though. Whatever he might have been thinking, he didn't say a word as he got to his feet and followed her out the back door.

Ridge trailed Marianne a good distance from the house until she stopped under the ancient oak everyone in the family seemed to gravitate to. When she turned to him, he nodded toward it. "I have to know what's so special about this tree."

Resting a hand on the gnarled trunk, she looked up through the branches with the kind of sad smile only women seemed to be able to manage. "This was my father's favorite spot on the farm. He and the boys used to eat lunch here, just as all the Sawyers did before them. Dad said it made him feel connected to his roots."

Ridge nodded. He admired the Sawyers' solid connection to their past—and to each other.

"You wanted to talk to me," he reminded her, opening his mind to whatever she had to say.

"I thought your mother was expecting you in Colorado."

"I called a few days ago to let her know I'm staying a while longer," he assured her. "Folks love riding in Betsy, so aerial tours are a big part of my business, especially when we get into the fall. I've got at least a dozen names from the picnic, and a little word of mouth goes a long way."

"You're planning to stay here, then."

"John said I can stay as long as I want, even bought me some earplugs to help with the snoring. In return, I'll help out around the farm, free of charge," he added to make it clear he wouldn't be taking advantage of the Sawyers' hospitality.

"Are you sure you want to do that? I mean, you told me you don't like to be in one place too long."

"You miss things that way."

"Such as?"

He shrugged. "Friends. Dogs. Having a place to come back to at the end of the day that doesn't charge you when you walk in the door."

"You like Harland, then?"

"Very much." There was plenty to like about the close-knit community on and around the farm. Because Ridge didn't know how to say that without spooking her, he settled on something less personal. "Little things mean a lot when you don't have them."

She eyed him with something resembling respect, which he took as a good sign. Marianne was by far the most mistrustful woman he'd ever met. He still wasn't sure why he was trying so hard to get through to her, and he had to wonder if his genetic stubbornness was steering him down a rocky, dead-end road.

"Kyle and his friends live for football," she finally said, determination sharpening her usually gentle drawl. "They play other sports, but once football camp starts, everything revolves around that. They practice rain or shine, tired or not. The coaches start out easy, then gradually get tougher. August first they start real practices, and with the heat they can get brutal."

Ridge grinned. "I remember. Something tells me you didn't play football, though. How do you know all this?"

"I'm the team mom, so I'm always there."

"Don't you have enough to do already?" he asked with a frown.

"Yes, but someone needs to be in charge of the

sidelines. The kids love the game, and so do the coaches. They sacrifice most of their free time to volunteer, and they do a great job. Getting a bunch of young kids to focus long enough to teach them teamwork and plays takes someone with the discipline of a drill sergeant and the patience of a saint."

She was starting to sound condescending, and his back went up. "I get that. What's your point?"

"You don't have children."

"So?"

"Coaching them is like herding cats. And there are two girls on the team," she added.

"Cool," he said without reservation, because he meant it. "I bet they hit hard and run fast."

Marianne just blinked at him, and he met her disbelieving look with an even one of his own. As soon as Kyle mentioned it, Ridge knew this coaching opportunity was one of those little things he'd talked about missing. Being connected to a community, at least for a little while, would be good for him. Besides, it sounded like fun.

Marianne looked so upset, he wanted to take her hands and reassure her. He managed to resist the urge, but it was tough.

"I understand why you're worried," he said, "but I can handle it. If I have trouble, I'll ask the other coaches or John for advice. I really want to help out."

Staring up at him, she shook her head. "Why?"

Searching his mind, he stumbled on words that more or less summed up his reasoning. "Because it will matter to the kids and their families. I probably met some of them at the wedding and the picnic, and they seem like good people. I wanna make sure they get a football season."

"It's a ton of work you won't get paid for. What's in it for you?"

A place to belong, he wanted to say. He'd been searching for one all his life, and Harland felt like it might be the one. Instinct told him that it was too intense an emotion to share with this woman he barely knew. "I like new challenges."

She assessed him with a long, thoughtful look, and he could hear the mom wheels spinning in her head. Understanding her reluctance, he endured her scrutiny with what he hoped came across as confidence. She was concerned about his disappointing her son and his friends, and Ridge couldn't blame her.

Being new in town, he was aware that folks wouldn't take to him right away, much less trust him with their children. If Marianne went out on a limb and vouched for him, they'd accept him without question. This was a big risk for her to take, but he hoped she'd let him prove he was worth it.

Finally, she held out her hand and they shook.

"I'll talk to the head coach. I just hope you know what you're getting yourself into."

He chuckled. "Not a clue, but I learn fast. I'll figure it out."

The look she gave him said she had her doubts, but he gave her credit for not saying so out loud.

Sunday morning, Marianne was waiting for John and the kids when she heard footsteps on the back porch. Ridge staggered through the back door with Tucker on his heels, and she didn't bother to hide her surprise.

The dog flopped down on the floor beside her, and she turned a page in the newspaper. "You're up early for a Sunday."

"Church," he said in a gruff morning voice as he groped along the counter to reach the coffeemaker.

After the brush-off she'd gotten the first Sunday he was with them, his comment astonished her. "I must still be dreaming. It sounded like you said you were coming to church with us."

"I am. First, I need coffee."

"Help yourself."

She laughed, and for some reason he gave her a slow grin.

"What?" she asked.

"You have a great laugh. You should laugh more."

While the compliment settled into a cozy place, she asked, "You're really going to church?"

Blowing on his coffee, he nodded. "When I was at the team meeting yesterday, Coach made it clear he expects to see me there. Guy as big as that, you don't argue when he tells you to do something."

"That's not a good reason to go," she argued, offended that he'd even consider attending services for such a transparent reason.

"I was kidding, Marianne. He suggested I go as a way to get to know the families, but he didn't make it an order or anything." Flashing a mischievous grin, he added, "Who knows? It might even be good for me."

"I don't doubt that for a second," she said primly.

Before she could begin a proper lecture, the kids pounded down the steps, freshly scrubbed and dressed. When he heard them, John clicked the TV off and sauntered in from the living room.

"Rotten Braves," he muttered. "They're killing me this season."

"Again," Ridge taunted him. "My Rockies, on the other hand, are in first place."

To Marianne's complete amazement, he rinsed out his cup and put it in the dishwasher. All by himself, without her asking. Glancing up, she wondered if an angel had landed on his shoulder sometime during the night and was whispering in his ear. Whatever the reason, she decided she liked the change.

When they got outside, Ridge opened the back door for the kids, and then the driver's door for her. Marianne was so stunned by the gesture, she didn't move.

"Everything okay?" he asked, looking confused.

"Don't you want to drive?"

"Your car, you drive," he said as if it hadn't even occurred to him to think otherwise.

Peter always drove, she recalled bitterly. Even her car, even when he didn't know where they were going and she did. Then again, during their marriage Peter was in charge of more than the driving. Assertive to the core, he naturally took over. She'd convinced herself he couldn't help it, any more than a shy man could help being quiet. Ridge was just as assertive, she realized, but he didn't assume he'd be in charge of every situation. She couldn't help noticing—and appreciating—the difference.

During the short ride to church, Kyle and Emily repeated the verses they'd memorized for Bible study. They were short and simple, but strung together they made a pleasant beginning to the day.

Do not be afraid, for I am with you.
Love your neighbor as yourself.

Let all that you do be done in love.

"That's one of my favorites," Marianne told them as she turned into the parking lot. "It always makes me think of my mother."

"Gramma's in heaven with Granddad," Emily informed them in a very grown-up voice. "Aunt Lisa says they watch us from up there and smile."

"I'm sure they do." Ridge looked back at them. "They're real proud of you two."

"And Mommy, too," Emily prompted.

Turning to her with an admiring smile, he nodded. "And Mommy, too. Especially Mommy."

He didn't touch her, but his words flowed over Marianne like a caress. This was a side of him she hadn't expected to find beneath all those rough edges. Kind and caring, he had a way of reaching people and making them feel important. He'd accomplished that amazing feat with her kids the first day they met him. It was easy to see they were getting very attached to this man who was always willing to drop what he was doing and make time for them.

Whether it was running plays with Kyle or memorizing the names of Emily's extended family of dolls, Ridge showed an interest in everything they did. They treasured his attention in a way that made Marianne realize that she'd been fooling herself thinking she could fill the roles of both mother and father for them.

Pleasant as things were now, she worried about how devastated they'd be when he got bored with quiet little Harland and flew off to his next adventure. She wished she could protect her kids from the pain that losing him would cause them, but it was too late for that. When the time came for him to go, they'd have to cope with their disappointment as best they could.

That included her, Marianne realized with sudden clarity. The revelation didn't settle well, but she had to be honest with herself. She'd miss him when he was gone.

Ridge couldn't remember the last time he'd set foot in a church.

It wasn't that he was against religion. Raised with a healthy respect for the Almighty, Ridge worshipped not in a church, but out in the open. He felt closest to God when he was flying, soaring above the clouds where the sun was the brightest.

When he was young, his mother would point out how rays of sunlight sometimes plunged through the clouds to meet the ground. She used to tell him that was God opening a door and extending a stairway so souls could find their way into heaven. The poetic notion had always appealed to

Ridge much more than being stuck inside singing and listening to sermons.

But this morning he found himself in a quaint Carolina chapel, watching Pastor Charles work his way through the congregation on his way to what looked like a hand-carved oak pulpit. Ridge had met the friendly man at Matt and Caty's wedding, which made him slightly less uncomfortable. Still, he couldn't shake the feeling that every person there knew he'd rather be out flying.

"Don't worry," Matt whispered from beside him. "It gets easier."

"Thanks."

His buddy had recently reformed, so Ridge hoped Matt knew what he was talking about. When the opening chords of the first hymn echoed from the organ in back, the song sounded vaguely familiar. Emily tapped his arm and offered him a hymnal.

"It's been a while," he confided, smiling down at her. "Will you help me out?"

Nodding, she climbed onto the pew and into his arms. She settled in and pointed out the page they were on.

While he held this precious little girl and tried to match her clear, sweet pitch, Ridge felt something completely unexpected. Like a wave, it began gently, slowly moving over him until he felt like he'd been wrapped in warm air. That feeling nestled into the deepest corner of his heart, one he'd been neglecting for a long, long time.

Unnerved, he glanced at Emily, but she didn't seem to notice it. She just looked back at him with those innocent blue eyes and smiled. When the song was finished, he figured she'd want to rejoin her brother, so he started to put her down. She wrapped her arms around him and held on tight, and he couldn't resist returning the affectionate gesture.

Glancing up at the beautiful stained-glass window hanging over the simple altar, Ridge noticed that it was a scene of Jesus surrounded by animals and children. It suited the little white church—and Harland—perfectly. While he stared at it, the baffling sensation he'd been feeling settled in even more deeply. It made him wonder if Emily wasn't the only one glad to have him in church this morning.

When the last chord died away, Pastor Charles opened his arms and trailed a fatherly look through the crowd, connecting with them in a way that made each person feel that he was thrilled to see them. When he saw Ridge, his eyes lit up in surprise, then crinkled in a smile that could have melted a glacier.

"Welcome, one and all, on this beautiful morning. Since I hear there's rain on the way, I'll try to keep things short so our farming neighbors can get back to their harvesting." A murmur of appreciation went through the rows, and he continued. "So let's get right to one of my favorite subjects. Family."

Everyone laughed except Ridge, and Matt leaned in to explain. "He and his wife had six kids of their own and adopted four more. Their youngest goes to school with Kyle."

Ridge was impressed. The pastor looked to be in his early sixties, and it would take an incredibly generous couple to adopt such a young child at that age. While Ridge digested that, he noticed someone move off to his left. Charlie Simmons gave him a discreet wave, nodding his approval.

"You're the golden boy," Matt said with a chuckle. "Whole town's talking about it."

"How would you know?" Ridge murmured. "You work all the time."

"Caty told me."

Ridge glanced down the row and was rewarded with one of Mrs. Sawyer's bright smiles. As he returned the gesture, it hit him.

He belonged here.

Thinking back, he couldn't recall a time when he'd been anywhere long enough to feel totally comfortable. When he was a kid, Ridge's family had moved around almost continuously. Between his father's inability to keep a job and angry landlords demanding back rent, he and his parents never lived anywhere more than a year. Mom always kept her special treasures packed away, knowing they'd be moving on before long. To this day, she hated packing.

Their nomadic lifestyle had made it tough for Ridge to settle in at school, and he became adept at gliding along, earning decent grades without calling too much attention to himself. In high school he'd been the new kid from Colorado with the funny name, and it marked him as an outsider. Quarterbacking a winning football team had helped a little, but not enough. Those kids had all grown up together, and there wasn't room in their tight circle for him. By the time he graduated, moving around had more or less become a habit. He'd made it work for him by becoming a pilot and seeing as much of the world as he could take in.

Not once in his entire life had he belonged somewhere. Discovering that the folks in Harland had embraced him as one of their own should have made him feel good.

In reality, it was more confusing than anything. His own mother insisted he had a Gypsy's heart, since he was happiest when he was on the move. But standing there with Emily in his arms, Ridge wondered if maybe it was time to come in for a landing.

Chapter Five

July 10 dawned clear and warm, promising to become hot and humid by the time camp ended at noon. Both kids were wired, Kyle anxious for football to start—finally—and Emily just as excited by her new role with the rookie cheer squad. Too young to participate, she'd charmed her way into the heart of the twenty-year-old coach last year. This season, Emily had the very official title of cheerleading assistant. They had no idea what that meant, but Marianne knew that being acknowledged as part of the team was what mattered to Emily.

Marianne couldn't imagine where Ridge had gotten to, but Betsy was gone so she figured he must be working. They were supposed to leave at eight-thirty, though. Where was he? By quarter after, she was muttering to herself while she finished packing up. The first day was always chaotic, and she found it went better if she took charge of the snacks.

"Made a promise." Frustrated, she jammed a few more water bottles into the ice-filled cooler and slammed the cover shut. "Kids are depending on him, and where is he?"

"Right here," Ridge answered from the doorway, making her jump.

"Don't do that," she scolded. "Make some noise or something. I can hear John coming from half a mile away."

"Didn't you hear Betsy?" The way he said it, he could have been talking about a gabby old aunt.

"I was too busy to notice. I've gotten so used to you taking off and landing, I don't hear her anymore."

A grin slowly spread across his face. By the time he was done, it was absolutely devastating. Even though she knew perfectly well she was tempting fate, she couldn't make herself look away.

"That's good, right?" he asked.

It was a simple enough question, but she didn't know how to respond. When Ridge first showed up in his flying museum, she thought he'd be leaving in a few days. The idea of becoming accustomed to his presence—and his plane's—hadn't occurred to her. Now that it had happened, she wasn't sure how she felt about it.

"Is that a yes?" He cocked his head, reminding her of Tucker hinting for a treat.

"I—I guess," she stammered. "It's fine."

"I'll take fine."

The mischief glinting in his eyes told her he enjoyed throwing her off balance, which she didn't appreciate. Much. Fortunately, he redeemed himself by picking up the heavy cooler and taking it out to the van for her. The man would test the resolve of a saint, she thought with a sigh. Too bad she was only human.

She'd just opened her mouth to call the kids when she heard them coming down the stairs. The players wouldn't be in pads and helmets today, but Kyle had on last year's game jersey. Emily was wearing a pleated lavender skirt and T-shirt she'd picked out because they were like the cheerleaders' uniforms. With a purple bow tied around her high ponytail, she looked ready for action.

"Look at you two," she approved, taking her camera out of the drawer.

"Aw, Mom," Kyle protested.

"Just one, I promise."

"Okay, but we gotta go or we're gonna be late."

"We can't be late, Mommy," Emily chimed in. "The team needs me."

To avoid just such a disaster, Marianne always scheduled in fifteen extra minutes. They both knew that, but she decided not to spoil their excitement by reminding them.

Marianne smiled at their enthusiasm while she snapped their picture. After taking an extra for good measure, she checked the digital display. "Got it. Ready?"

"Ready!" they shouted together, making a beeline for the van.

Marianne followed after them, astonished by what she saw. She'd stacked lawn chairs and her bin of spare equipment next to the van, figuring she'd load it while the kids got settled in their seats. Instead, she found everything in its place and both sliding doors open. Ridge stood next to the driver's door like a valet.

"What's this?" she asked.

"I was late, so I wanted to make up for it." Bowing, he motioned to her seat.

Marianne got in and smiled when he closed the door for her. She thanked him through the open window.

"You're welcome." Peering in Emily's door, he grinned. "Look at you, sweetness. You gonna show all those older girls how it's done?"

Eyes sparkling at the special nickname he'd given her, Emily beamed. "You betcha!"

Ridge rolled the door closed and climbed into the passenger seat beside Marianne. She still wasn't used to having another adult in the car with her, so it felt a little strange. Shrugging off her discomfort, she rolled up the windows, turned on the A/C and headed down the driveway.

The practice field was fifteen minutes away. To keep the kids from bouncing through the roof, Marianne plugged in her iPod so Kyle and Emily could sing along with their favorite new tunes. She glanced over to find Ridge with his head buried in his coach's manual. For the first time since she'd met him, he seemed unsure of himself. Charlie Simmons's rigorous coaching requirements didn't seem to faze him, but the prospect of working with a bunch of kids clearly had him rattled.

Hoping to ease his mind, she said, "You won't need that today. Mostly, you'll be sorting through the talent and learning which face goes with which name."

His head flew up, his expression one of pure horror. "Names? I never even thought of that." He spun backward to look at Kyle. "How many of you are there?"

"Coach said twenty-three, but there might be a couple more after camp starts. We're always looking for more players."

"Twenty-three kids," Ridge murmured, looking a little pale.

"Don't worry," Marianne reassured him. "We

put their names on their shirts with fabric tape. When they start with helmets, we label those, too. By the time the season starts, you'll know them all."

"What about the Perkins twins?" he asked. "They must look alike."

"Justin got a crew cut, and Jimmy dyed his hair blue and gold," Kyle informed him. "No problem."

"Blue and gold, huh?" Ridge commented. "Now that's team spirit. I got a feeling I'm gonna like that kid."

During the rest of the drive, Kyle went through the roster, giving Ridge hints on how to keep them all straight. When they arrived at the field, Marianne bypassed the parking area and continued along the dirt path the field manager used for his equipment truck.

"How come you get such a great spot?" Ridge asked.

"Team mom," she replied. "I've got all the gear, so I get VIP parking."

"Where'd you get so much stuff?"

"When the season's over, I go around to the parents and collect cleats and any other equipment they bought that won't fit next year," she explained as she parked in the shade of a maple tree. "Folks can take what they need out of the bin so they don't have to buy everything new. Sports equipment is expensive, and sometimes getting it for free means the difference between a kid playing or not."

"Great idea. I'd hate to have kids miss out because they couldn't afford the gear."

She'd expect him to be more concerned about the team losing a talented player, so his comment impressed her. He really understood that this was about what football meant to the kids, not the other way around.

This man was just full of surprises.

The kid was a natural.

Proud as any father watching from the stands, Ridge marveled at Kyle's speed in the flat, the crispness of his patterns and the fact that he never dawdled. No matter how far out he'd run, he always trotted back to his place, ready for the next drill.

Ridge had to remind himself to keep an eye on the others, too. Since Ridge had played quarterback, Charlie had asked him to work with their potential receivers and running backs and highlight the best candidates. Five of them stood out—players like Kyle who could manage a basic pattern and weren't too bothered by the heat.

The younger ones were dropping like flies, though. Whenever one of them started to stagger, Marianne swooped in and walked the kid off the field to the chairs she'd set up in the shade. After getting them some water and spritzing them with a spray bottle, she made sure they were good to go and sent them back in. She didn't baby them, he noticed, but she wasn't heartless, either. Obviously, Kyle had trained her well.

During a water break, Ridge looked around at the teams set up in the other three corners of the huge field. The flag footballers were basically learning how to stand still and listen, while the three older teams were already walking through patterns. All four cheerleading squads were nearby, and occasionally their chanting drifted in on the breeze. They weren't quite in sync yet, but the girls looked like they were having a blast.

Taking another swig of water, Ridge noticed a kid leaning on the fence that surrounded the field. Openly interested, he was watching the drills intently. Taller than the other kids, he had the in-between look of a little boy rapidly growing into a bigger one. Ridge had a tough time gauging kids, but he pegged him at around Kyle's age.

He was dressed in well-worn shorts and sneakers, his T-shirt clean but faded. Ridge recalled the look well. Poor but proud. It was like seeing a picture of himself twentysomething years ago. As if that weren't enough, his gut told him this boy wanted to play. That was really all he needed to know.

Ridge sauntered over and leaned on the gate near their visitor. "Hey there. I'm Coach Collins."

The kid hesitated, then stuck his hand over the fence. "I'm Danny Hodges. Nice to meet you, sir."

Those careful manners came straight from Mom, Ridge knew. He recognized so much of himself in Danny, it was hard not to pull him onto the field and pop a pair of cleats on his feet. Big feet, he noticed with a quick glance down. He wondered if Marianne had anything Danny's size in her bin. If not, the problem was easy enough to solve with a trip to the local sports shop.

Whoa now, he cautioned himself. *First you should ask him if he wants to play.*

"So." Leaning back so he'd look casual, Ridge sipped from his water bottle. "What brings you by?"

Danny indicated a woman sitting in the stands. "My babysitter's sons both play. I'm here with them."

"Oh, yeah? Which ones?"

"The twins. Jimmy and Justin." He pointed them out on the field. "They're really good."

Ridge gave him a quick once-over and grinned. "I'll bet you'd be good, too, if we got you out there."

Danny swallowed hard and firmed his brave little-boy chin. "That's nice of you to say, sir, but I can't."

Ridge leaned close, like he was sharing a secret. "Y'know, when I was your age, I wanted to play football more than anything. I thought I couldn't 'cause we didn't have the money for it. Then the coach told me there were some scholarships, and if I worked real hard, he'd make sure I got one."

"Really?" Danny's dark eyes glittered with interest, and he looked up at Ridge like he was the latest superhero. "Do you think maybe Coach Simmons has one of those for me?"

Touchdown.

Ridge swung the gate open and stood back to let Danny through. "Tell you what? Come on in and show me what you got. Then we'll talk about that scholarship."

If they didn't exist, Ridge vowed to invent one. In his mind, no kid who wanted to play should ever be left standing on the sidelines.

Kyle and Emily were devouring slices of watermelon while Marianne made sandwiches for lunch. When Ridge pulled open a drawer and slipped in a small stack of twenties, she gave him the eye.

"What are you doing?"

"Paying the fee for Danny Hodges," he said quietly. "I told him there was a scholarship, and he won it today. Charlie agreed to back up my story, but I want to cover it in cash so nobody finds out it was me. I know I can trust you."

Considering his vagabond lifestyle, she was stunned to hear those words come out of his mouth. She was also honored. He trusted her. She had no idea why that meant so much to her, but it pleased her immensely.

"Did you see that Danny Hodges run?" Ridge asked in his normal voice as he took the fresh pitcher of lemonade from the fridge. He poured out glasses for the kids, then for Marianne and himself. "He's like a colt who came out of nowhere to run the Kentucky Derby. We just have to get him trained and into the starting gate."

"Wait a minute." Marianne stopped spreading mayo and held up a hand to slow him down. "Are you talking about the boy who needed size-seven cleats?"

"The same. He's amazing, isn't he, Kyle?" he added, turning to his adoring sidekick for support.

"Real fast," Kyle agreed around a mouthful of melon. After swallowing, he went on. "I was talking to him on a break, and he said he and his mom just moved here. He's gonna be in my grade, so I introduced him around to the guys. He's cool."

It was so like her son, Marianne thought proudly. It would never occur to him that making the new kid feel welcome was anything out of the ordinary. He did it because he was Kyle.

She caught a flash of movement outside and saw an unfamiliar hatchback drive around the circle to park next to the barn. A slender woman stepped out, pulling back when Tucker loped over to greet her. He did his exuberant glad-to-meet-you dance, then sat and wagged his tail for attention. After a few seconds, she relaxed enough to reach down and pet him.

"Now, who could that be?" Marianne asked, thinking the woman looked terrified as she made her way toward the house. "Poor thing. She's probably lost and wondering where civilization is."

Wiping her hands on a towel, Marianne smiled and opened the back door. "Can we help you?"

"Yes, ma'am," their visitor said in a voice so faint, Marianne could barely hear her. "I'm looking for Coach Collins."

Ridge joined them at the door, wearing an unnervingly charming smile. "I'm Ridge Collins," he said, extending his hand.

The woman hesitated, but he didn't withdraw

his hand. When she finally accepted the friendly gesture, he went on. "What can I do for you?"

"I'm Pamela Hodges," she said a little more forcefully. "Danny's mother."

Uh-oh. Marianne knew that tone, had heard it on the sidelines plenty of times. It was the sound of an unhappy parent. She was curious to see how Ridge would handle the awkward situation.

"I'm glad you came by. It's great to meet you."

He sounded as if he really meant it. From his reaction, Marianne guessed that he'd been expecting the visit and was actually looking forward to it. More proof that the man was insane.

"I have some concerns about Danny playing football." A flinty look came into Pamela's soft gray eyes. Protecting her son made her bolder, Marianne noted with admiration. Timid as she seemed at first glance, this woman had a streak of mama grizzly in her.

"Is there someplace private we could talk?" Pamela asked, glancing at the kids who were trying to look as if they weren't listening. They weren't fooling anyone, but Marianne silently praised them for the effort.

Opening the door, Ridge stepped out and motioned her ahead of him. He ushered her to what they all called Ethan's tree, and Marianne had to smile. She wondered if he was hoping to get a little help from a wise old farmer he'd never met but openly admired.

Pamela stopped and turned to him, her expression hardened by determination. Her voice filtered in through the screen door, but Marianne couldn't hear anything beyond the tone. She couldn't hear Ridge's voice at all.

Trying not to eavesdrop, Marianne filled a bowl with chips and set everything on the table. She sat down and started on her sandwich, then snuck a look out the window. Arms folded, Ridge seemed to just be listening, nodding here and there.

It didn't look good.

After several minutes, Pamela apparently ran out of things to say. Marianne could relate to the perplexed look the woman gave Ridge before she offered up a tentative smile and went on her way. When Ridge came back inside, he was smiling, too.

"You worked your magic on that poor woman, didn't you?" Marianne asked.

She'd meant to scold him for it, but it came out sounding almost proud. As a teacher, she knew Danny was the kind of kid who could slip through the cracks, missing out simply because his mother couldn't afford things beyond the basics. School was important, but it could only get him so far. While he was by nature a great kid, Kyle had benefited tremendously from learning to work as part of a team.

Unlike his father, she added bitterly before she could stop herself. Too late, she'd discovered that Peter was an egomaniac, completely ignorant of how his self-centered attitude affected those around him. If she accomplished anything in her life, she wanted to make sure her children were very far removed from that kind of selfishness.

"Not exactly," Ridge began, joining them at the table. "She's got some legitimate concerns and wanted to talk to me about them, face-to-face. See what kinda guy I am," he added with a playful grin.

Marianne caught herself before she responded to that smile, but just barely. To avoid temptation, she picked up her lemonade. "And?"

"I told her we really need him and she'd be doing the team a big favor letting Danny play. That's why he got the scholarship. She said school comes first, which Charlie and I totally agree with. Mrs. Perkins is his babysitter, so he can ride to practices with her. No problem."

In the short time she'd known him, Marianne had learned this was Ridge's approach to life in general. When he hit an obstacle, he circled it for a while, considering all the angles until he figured a way around it. As if his rugged good looks and quick mind weren't enough, beneath it all beat a kind and generous heart.

Much as she hated to admit it, the cocky pilot was beginning to grow on her.

Chapter Six

Sunday was game day.

Opening game day, to be precise. After four grueling weeks of work, it was time for the kids to put what they'd learned into practice against another team. To make sure everything ran smoothly, Marianne got up an hour earlier than usual. Two coolers, bowls of frozen fruit for snacks, and the first aid kit went into the van before breakfast. The kids could barely eat, but she forced some oatmeal and bananas on them, reminding them both to start hydrating.

Church came first, so they wouldn't be back before the game started at noon. The online weather channel predicted it would be a humid eighty-seven by then.

When she decided they'd eaten as much as was reasonable, she shooed them upstairs to get dressed. She was checking things off her list when

Ridge came through the back door with a shiny blue-and-gold gift bag in his hand.

"What's this?" she asked as he gave it to her.

"For you. From the team," he added quickly.

Wrapped in the tissue was a game jersey like the ones the players wore. On the front was the number one, and on the back it read WESTON. Totally baffled, she looked at him for an explanation.

"We wanted to thank you for all the time you put in. I hope you like it."

Something in his tone got her attention, and she grinned at him. "This was your idea."

"Well, yeah," he admitted slowly, as if he'd gotten caught doing something wrong. "But the other coaches and the kids thought it was cool."

It was such a thoughtful thing to do, she wasn't sure how to thank him properly. Stepping closer, she kissed his sunburned cheek. "It's very cool. Thank you."

"Sure."

They stood there for a few seconds just looking at each other, and she wondered if she'd overstepped some unspoken boundary with him. As her face warmed with embarrassment, she pulled back and searched for something to say. "You look nice. Ready for the big game, I mean."

The dark blue coach's shirt accented his broad

shoulders, and the gold in the Wildcats logo picked up the unusual color of his eyes.

"I didn't know you owned a watch," she said.

"Bought it yesterday," he confided, looking at it as if he wasn't quite comfortable wearing it. "I thought it might make me look more official."

She'd never seen the cocky pilot so unsure of himself. Marianne wouldn't have thought it possible, but that sliver of vulnerability made him even more appealing.

"You look completely official to me," she said as she pulled her new shirt on. "And I should know. I'm number one."

"Yes, you are." Eyes twinkling with approval, he leaned in to kiss her cheek. When he pulled away, he gave her a broad grin. "You're finally starting to like me, aren't you?"

It was easy to smile back. "Maybe just a little."

"Took you long enough," he grumbled. "Most women take to me right off, y'know."

Rolling her eyes, she laughed. "No doubt."

"Not you, though," he continued, leaning against the counter in a casual pose. "How come?"

"I'm very, very picky."

"Good. You should be."

Marianne couldn't for the life of her imagine what he meant by that. Unfortunately, before she could ask, she became distracted by Kyle and his tangled shoulder pads.

"All right, Wildcats," Charlie Simmons called out in his booming coach's voice. The team gathered around him, and he continued. "First game is always tough, but you've all worked hard, and you're ready. No matter who they line up opposite you, I want you to stand in there and hold your position. Watch each other's backs, and if you see a teammate struggling, help 'em out." He pointed across the field. "I want Kenwood to know they aren't playing twenty-five separate players. They're up against all of us as a team."

The players cheered, blowing some of the anxiety out of the nervous group. Ridge admired Charlie's concise, upbeat speech. It was one of the best he'd ever heard.

When the kids settled down, Charlie said, "Hands in, everybody."

Coaches and players each put a hand into the circle like the spokes of a wheel and bowed their heads. Although he'd been going to church on a regular basis, Ridge still wasn't big on praying in public. He felt a little awkward doing it, but judging by the size of the Kenwood players, the Wildcats could use all the help they could get.

"Heavenly Father," Charlie began, "please watch

over everyone on this field today. Keep them safe and help them to be proud of their efforts—win or lose. Amen."

The group murmured their response, and Charlie lifted his head. He connected with each kid in turn, then grinned at the whole group. "Now go out there and give me everything you've got."

With a shrill war cry that could only come from kids whose voices hadn't changed yet, they stampeded toward their end zone to wait for team introductions. Their excitement was contagious.

Ridge could almost feel the weight of his old helmet and shoulder pads, the new cleats his mother somehow always managed to buy. He didn't know where the money came from, but even when he was young he knew she'd gone without something to get them for him. Thinking about that made him smile. She'd called earlier to wish him luck.

"Make sure you record that game so I can see it," she'd added.

That was Mom, he mused as he strapped his digital recorder to the fence near midfield. No matter where he was or what he was doing, she was always behind him a hundred percent.

As the announcer called the name and number of the first Wildcat, the hometown crowd jumped to their feet and went crazy. Ridge was thrilled to hear the same raucous support for everyone, from first-years to returning favorites. He had a hunch there'd be a few cases of laryngitis around town tomorrow.

"Number 44," the announcer shouted, "Kyle Weston!"

The cheering ratcheted up a notch as Kyle calmly trotted out. He didn't dance or hold out his arms as if they'd already won. He just joined his teammates on the fifty-yard line and turned to cheer for the next kid. Watching him made Ridge's heart swell with pride. Kyle wasn't his son, but football had forged a strong bond between them. Sharing this moment with Kyle meant the world to Ridge.

Up in the stands, he found Marianne, clapping for all she was worth and shouting for each kid. She'd snaked her ponytail through the opening in the back of her hat, and the sun picked up the strands of honey in her hair. When she noticed him, her eyes were a shining, delighted blue he'd never seen. Then he realized they were filled with tears of joy.

Thank you, she mouthed.

He'd never seen such raw emotion from a woman at a football game. Often, they were texting or reading or looking around, completely bored. But this was a mother watching her son doing what he loved. When Ridge had offered to help with the team, he knew how important it was to Kyle. It hadn't occurred to him that it would mean just as much to Marianne. The warmth in her gaze dove deep inside him, nudging itself into that place he'd felt while holding Emily this morning in church.

Suddenly, Ridge wished he was standing beside Marianne, sharing this with her. Since that wasn't possible, he nodded and grinned back. The brilliant smile he got in return just about knocked him off his feet, and that was when he knew.

The beautiful and very complicated Marianne Weston had gotten under his skin. He was in big, big trouble.

Ruthy's Place was packed.

After beating the Kenwood Falcons 24–18, the entire Wildcats team and their fans descended on the diner, quickly filling it to capacity.

Ruthy was prepared, Marianne noticed, from extra waitstaff to tables on the back deck and extra chairs around the bistro tables out front. Still, she hoped nobody was counting noses. The diner's maximum capacity was 200, and she wouldn't be surprised if they'd gone beyond that. Then she saw the fire marshal at the counter, clapping his grandson on the back while they waited for ice cream. Apparently, town fire codes were the furthest thing from his mind today.

Luckily, the four of them had seats at one of the tables reserved for the team. Some folks were hanging around outside, waiting for their turn to order. Lisa paused only long enough to high-five her nephew.

"Awesome game! Those Kenwood coaches will think twice next time they play you guys."

After zooming around the group to scribble down their orders, she rushed toward the kitchen to get them in line. A quick glance around showed Marianne that Lisa and the other waitresses were wearing sneakers instead of their usual 1940s-style shoes. Smart girls. Even with the extra help Ruthy had scheduled, by the time everyone left, those girls would feel like they'd run a marathon.

"To our first win," Ridge said, clinking glasses with her and the kids. Turning to Pamela Hodges, he generously included her and Danny. "Thanks for being a part of it."

"We're gonna have seven more," Danny informed him with a grin. "We're going undefeated."

Ridge chuckled. "You keep running the way you did today, we just might."

"Thanks again for helping him, Coach Collins," Pamela said.

"Danny does the hard part, believe me. And it's

Ridge," he added with that bright, friendly grin that seemed to be wired into his personality.

Smiling, Pamela blushed and looked away to rearrange her silverware. It was painfully obvious that the shy woman had caught a bit of her son's hero worship. Marianne had gotten used to having Ridge to herself, and she was just human enough to admit she didn't like sharing him with another woman.

Suddenly, she realized he was giving her an odd look.

"You okay?" he asked.

"Sure. Just wondering how many people are here." She did a quick scan of the crowd.

"A bunch, that's for sure." His eyes cruised toward the door, and he frowned. "I think that dude is seriously lost."

Marianne followed his nod toward a tall man wearing a designer suit and tie. Apprehension snaked up her spine, but she forced herself to meet those dark, incisive eyes. He smiled, but it was a cool gesture without a shred of warmth in it. She didn't want him pushing through the crowd to their table, so she motioned for him to wait outside.

"I know him," she explained as she stood. "I'll go give him directions."

Ridge's brow folded into a scowl. "Is something wrong? You're white as a sheet."

"I'm fine." Thankfully, Lisa showed up with their food, distracting him. "You stay here with the kids. I'll be right back."

Ridge had never seen Marianne pushed off-stride, but she looked downright shaken as she weaved her way through the jam-packed dining room. Their overdressed visitor greeted her, then opened the door for her to go ahead of him. From where Ridge sat, their reunion looked chillier than Glacier Bay in January.

Emily didn't seem to notice the exchange, but Kyle stared hard, not even bothering to cover his displeasure. Put simply, the kid looked furious. It was a stark contrast to the laughing conversation he'd been having with his teammates just a minute before.

Ridge was about to ask what was going on when Emily tapped his arm. "May I have the ketchup, please?"

"Sure, sweetness."

He handed it to her and made sure she had a couple of napkins covering her cheerleader's skirt. He was no expert, but he figured it would be murder to get red stains out of the pleated white fabric. When she was set, he forked up some coleslaw and leaned to his left.

"Who's the suit?" he asked without looking at Kyle. It would give the boy a chance to ignore him if he'd rather. After a few awkward seconds, Kyle sighed.

"My father."

Ridge almost choked. He carefully finished his mouthful of coleslaw, chasing it with a long slug of water.

"I think that's pretty much how Mom feels, too," Kyle said quietly.

Emily was engrossed in a Barbie debate with one of her friends, completely unaware that anything was wrong.

Eyeing Kyle, Ridge asked, "How long has it been since you saw him?"

"Five years, I guess. He left when Emmy was a baby, and we haven't seen him since."

Ridge had heard pieces of this story already, but he was still appalled that Peter Weston had simply turned his back on his wife and children. "How'd you know it was him?"

Kyle gave him a "get real" look, and he acknowledged it with a halfhearted chuckle. "Right. Sorry. You okay with him being here?"

The kid shrugged, which Ridge had learned meant he didn't like something but recognized there was nothing he could do about it. "As long as he doesn't upset Mom, I don't care."

Trying to look nonchalant, Ridge let his gaze wander to the tense scene framed by the side window. Judging by Marianne's stiff posture, she was more than upset. He tried reading their lips but couldn't piece together what they were saying.

One thing he knew for sure. It wasn't good.

"What are you doing here?" Marianne snarled, glancing around to be sure no one could hear them. Ruthy's sidewalk, smack in the center of town, wasn't the place she'd have chosen for this out-of-the-blue reunion. Since Peter hadn't given her a choice, she figured it was as good a place as any to make her stand. She'd fought long and hard to get past the humiliation he'd dumped on her. She wasn't about to let him drag her back into the mud.

"I went by the farm but no one was home. When I drove back through town, I saw all the cars and thought you might be here. I want to see Kyle," he added in the smooth, educated voice that had charmed her so completely the first time she met him. "It's been a long time, and I miss him."

"You don't even know him," she seethed, grateful that the kids were facing away from the window. Feeling the heat in her face, she knew she looked furious.

"I know," he admitted with a sigh. "I'd like to change that."

As she struggled to get her mind wrapped around the fact that Peter was here, she tried to recall the last time she'd seen him. It was an afternoon in the park, and things had been very strained between them. While Kyle had been doing his best imitation of a monkey on the jungle gym, she and Peter had circled the playground with Emily's stroller. Marianne recalled trying to come up with things to talk about. Even then, she suspected that the man who'd promised to love her until the end of his life had completely lost interest in her. And Emily.

"What about your daughter?" she demanded. "Have you missed her, too?"

"She was just a baby," he scoffed. "She doesn't even know who I am."

"She knows you left us, that you didn't want her."

Or me, Marianne added silently. That prick of pain returned, but it wasn't as strong as it used to be. While she couldn't help wondering what had changed, she cautioned herself to stay focused. If she didn't, Peter would overwhelm her completely and she'd turn into a stammering moron.

She wasn't the same timid, compliant doormat he'd married. He would find that out soon enough.

The thought gave her some confidence, and she glared at him while he made an obvious attempt to calm her down.

"Honey, you know things weren't good between us. If I'd stayed, I'd just have been delaying the inevitable."

"When people have marriage trouble," she informed him forcefully, "they at least try to work things out. Especially when they have children."

He took a step toward her, closing the distance she'd purposefully set between them. "Would you have tried?"

His implication was insulting, and she fought to keep her voice steady. "Of course. You never gave me the chance."

He seemed to chew on that for a few seconds, then shrugged. "That's water under the bridge now. I still want to see Kyle."

Not in this lifetime, she wanted to snap, but she caught herself. "That's not my decision," she said in her most reasonable tone. "It's his."

Peter glanced through the window with a frown. "Do you think he'll agree?"

"I have no idea, and as you can see, now's not a good time. Come out to the farm around four."

Not only would that get him off the sidewalk,

it would give Marianne time to brace herself for his visit. Despite her tough stance, his ambush had shaken her right down to her toes.

After considering that, he nodded and handed her an embossed business card. "My cell number is on there. I'm staying at the Executive Suites in Kenwood."

Of course he was. The quaint B&B outside Harland wasn't upscale enough for his taste. Ridge, on the other hand, had been perfectly willing to camp out on John's sofa for the last three months. She caught herself comparing the two of them and shook off the errant thought.

Hoping to sound as if she couldn't care less, she asked, "How long are you planning to stay?"

Peter's dark eyes narrowed, and she felt like she'd been sighted by a shark. A determined one. "Until I see my son."

As if on cue, they both turned and stalked in opposite directions. As Marianne entered the diner, she mentally congratulated herself. At least she hadn't just stood there watching him walk away from her.

"I don't wanna talk to him." Kyle met his mother's news with uncharacteristic stubbornness. "He ignored me all this time, now it's my turn to ignore him."

Marianne had put Ridge in charge of occupying Emily, and they were coloring at the table. Fortunately, Emily didn't seem the least bit interested in the tense conversation going on at the opposite end of the kitchen. Ridge, on the other hand, couldn't help listening in. He could relate to how Kyle felt, and it took everything he had not to interfere. But this was Marianne's family, so it was her decision. If it had been up to him, he'd have booted Peter Weston out of town without a second thought.

"You don't really mean to hurt your father," she reasoned.

"Yeah, I do. Let him see how he likes it." He folded his arms to emphasize what Ridge thought was a valid argument. That a ten-year-old kid was making it blew him away.

After a glance at Emily, Marianne focused back on Kyle. "I understand why you feel that way, but legally he has a right to see you."

"Aunt Caty's a lawyer," Kyle said hopefully. "Maybe she can make him go away."

Marianne's downcast expression told Ridge that one had stung. Kyle hadn't intended to insult her, but suggesting that she couldn't protect him from his father was a virtual slap in the face.

Forget keeping to himself, Ridge decided. It was time to speak up.

"This is America, Kyle," he said without looking up from the castle he was coloring. "You can't make anybody do anything."

"But it's not fair!"

"I know, but that's how it is. Your mom doesn't make the rules. She just follows them, like everybody else."

Kyle stomped from the kitchen and onto the back porch, whistling for Tucker.

"Be back by four!" Marianne called after him. It was no surprise he took off on his bike without acknowledging her.

Sighing, she turned to Ridge with a halfhearted smile. "Thanks for trying to help. I just don't know how to talk to him about this."

"Nobody would." With his bare foot, Ridge nudged a chair free for her. "Give him some space, and he'll be fine. Guys are like that."

"I suppose." Sitting down, she picked up a green crayon and started coloring in the hedges surrounding the princess's garden. After a few minutes, she sighed again. "Peter really caught me off guard."

Ridge had a few choice words about that, but held off out of respect for his feminine company. "My guess is that was his plan."

"It would be his style," she agreed in a pensive tone. "He likes to keep people guessing, says it gives him an edge in business. I used to like surprises," she added with a wry grin. "Not so much anymore."

Ridge recalled the look on her face when he landed in their cornfield, then again when he offered to help coach Kyle's team. Horrified came to mind. So did suspicious. Having seen her with her ex, it all made sense. The guy was intimidation dressed up in a nice suit.

Tentatively, he said, "Can I ask you something that's been bothering me for a while?"

"Sure." She propped her elbow on the table and rested her chin in her hand, resigned.

"If it's none of my business, just say so." She sighed, and he took that as a cue for him to go on. "This guy's obviously got money. What does he do?"

"He's a stockbroker."

Her tone made it clear that she disapproved, and he asked, "The legit kind?"

In response, she held her hand out and rocked it from side to side. "Even after we were married, I didn't know much about his business. Let's just say I heard him discussing things I wasn't thrilled about."

"If he's so successful, how is it you and the kids ended up with nothing?"

"His brother's a lawyer, and he drew up a prenup to 'protect Peter's business.'" Grimacing, she air-quoted the last few words. "It was standard, he said, so I took him at his word and signed it."

"Nice," Ridge growled. The Weston brothers had swindled Marianne and her children out of what should have rightly been theirs. "But there must be a child-support order or something."

"There is, but he won't pay it. I went to a lawyer in Charlotte, but his fee was outrageous, and he said I'd have to take Peter to court to make him comply." Her chin trembled, and a mist came into her eyes. "I just couldn't face all that, so I let it go."

She looked completely miserable, and Ridge wished he could ease her pain somehow. The man she'd loved had betrayed her and his own children in the worst possible way. "I think I see why it's so hard for you to trust me."

Marianne's stunned expression told him he'd nailed that one on the head. Sighing, she looked away without saying anything. Fortunately, Emily chose that moment to get all artistic on him.

"Ridge, can you draw an airplane in the sky? Right there, flying over that hill."

"Sure, sweetness."

"Blue and yellow," she clarified. "Like Betsy."

Her total lack of interest in what he and Marianne were saying made him grin. "I'm no Rembrandt, but I'll do my best."

"Thank you very much."

"No problem."

He chanced a look at Marianne, but she was focused on the flowers she was adding to the garden. Taking that as a hint to let the matter drop, he got to work on Emily's biplane. After several minutes, Marianne said his name. When he glanced up, she looked hesitant but forged ahead.

"I want to trust you," she confided. "It's hard."

Smiling reassurance, he nodded. "Yeah, it is. I'm doing my best to earn it, though."

Her sweet, shy smile gave him a glimpse of the girl she must have been once, before Peter's arrogance tore her apart.

"When we met," she began, "I thought there was no way I could ever like you. Tolerate you, maybe, but that was it."

"Yeah, sometimes I have that effect on people. They see the way I live and think I'm irresponsible. If they give me a chance to prove myself, they find out I'm as solid as they come."

He'd seen those incredibly blue eyes as cool as ice and blazing with fury. But as she studied him now, they shifted to a color he'd never seen. Like cornflowers, with a hint of purple. He wondered which emotion that particular hue was connected to.

"I really shouldn't like you," she said, shaking

her head. "There's nothing keeping you rooted to the ground."

"That's not entirely true," he heard himself saying. "I just need a good reason to stay."

In a startling flash he realized that Marianne, Kyle and Emily could keep him very happily grounded in Harland for the rest of his life.

The idea unnerved him, and Ridge pushed it away in self-defense. Even being married hadn't tamed his wanderlust, something he was still ashamed of. A year into their marriage, his wife had been miserable being alone while he flew all over the world. She'd begged him to quit the airline, or at least find a position that would keep him closer to home with her. In an attempt to make her happy, he'd switched to business shuttle runs back and forth among a handful of nearby cities. In a month, he was bored out of his skull and resumed his old schedule.

Six months later she was gone. Through a wash of tears she told him she loved him but couldn't keep waiting for him to come back, only to leave her again. It was his own fault, and Ridge had no intention of repeating that hurtful mistake. His failed marriage had taught him he wasn't the settling-down kind, and he couldn't drag a family from one state to the next. It might sound like a great adventure at first, but kids needed structure and school, a place to call home.

Ridge couldn't offer them anything but himself.

"Like lots of crayons." To cover his sudden discomfort, he started pawing through the box. Plucking one out, he read the name. "Blueberry. That'll work."

Now it was him avoiding Marianne's gaze. While he filled in the plane's fuselage, he hoped she'd just figure he was a complete loon.

Fortunately for everyone, Kyle returned much calmer than when he'd left. He came through the door and leaned down to rest his forehead on his mother's shoulder. "Sorry."

"That's okay." She reached an arm around him for a quick squeeze. "I know it's hard. Want something to drink?"

Nodding, he flopped onto the bench next to Ridge. "Fruit punch is fine."

"Coming up."

Giving him an encouraging smile, she got a glass and filled it with ice before adding some of the punch the kids seemed to drink by the gallon. She even stuck a lemon slice on the side before setting it in front of him.

The woman was amazing, Ridge thought with honest admiration. Nothing rattled her for long. Her quiet strength reminded him of his own mother, taking what life gave her and beating it down to make the road smoother for him.

Comparing Marianne to his mother was probably dangerous, so he cleared the unexpected thought from his mind.

"So, your dad's coming," he commented to neither kid in particular. "Pete, right?"

"Peter," Marianne corrected him primly, her lips pressed together. "He hates being called Pete."

"Is that right?" Hoping to lighten the mood, Ridge grinned. "I'll have to remember that."

She gave him a sharp look, but any response she might have made was lost in a throaty growl from the back porch. Through the door, Ridge saw Tucker lift his head, ears perked. When another growl came clearly through the screen, he couldn't help chuckling. "We've got company."

Too late, he realized how that must have sounded. Since he didn't technically live here, he should have said "You've got company." Nobody corrected him, though, which made him wonder if they all considered him part of the Sawyer gang. Part of him liked the idea of belonging here, having a place to call home. The restless part of him wasn't so sure.

While he was debating, a silver Jag convertible floated down the lane. The Sawyers' cars were next to the barn, but Peter ignored the obvious parking area and stopped right in front of the house blocking the lane. That was how city folks parked, Ridge thought with disdain. They didn't want to have to walk too far. The well-dressed man he'd seen at the diner stepped from the car and started toward the house.

Tucker leaped to his feet, hackles bristling while he barked a warning. Peter stopped in his tracks, clearly intimidated by the protective Lab. Tucker planted his front feet squarely on the top porch step, continuing to grumble like an angry wolf.

Distracted by the dog, it took Ridge a couple of seconds to register Marianne's reaction. Firming her chin, she pushed off from the table and stood like someone who'd been summoned for her own execution. He recognized it from the way his mother used to react when his father got home.

"I'm right here, Marianne," he said quietly to avoid upsetting Emily. "I won't let him hurt any of you."

Marianne gave him a long, confused look, then shook her head. "It wasn't like that."

"There are lots of ways to abuse somebody," he murmured. "It's just that some of them don't leave any marks."

The fear in her eyes told him he'd hit the mark, but Ridge let it go. Mom used to make up the same kind of excuses, trying to shield him from the brutal truth that had taken over their lives. Now Marianne was doing the same, to protect her own kids. It was the mother's instinct coming through, and he admired it more than he could ever say.

But if things with Peter got out of hand, Ridge would see it. And he was ready.

With a resigned sigh, Marianne opened the door to go out on the porch. "Good boy." She patted the Lab's head and smoothed her hand over the fur spiking up on his back. "Down, Tucker."

The dog wouldn't sit, but he did shift to the side so she could go down the steps. Alert for trouble, he finally sat but never took his eyes off their visitor. Ridge heard a quiet rumble of displeasure, as if Tucker were muttering to himself about how crazy she was to let this fancy stranger anywhere near her family. Ridge heartily agreed with him.

After a quick exchange, Peter followed Marianne up the steps, keeping a wary eye on the dog. Once he was inside, Tucker planted himself in front of the screen door. Apparently, he intended to stay right there until the man left.

Peter stood awkwardly at the door, sending Kyle a tentative smile. "Hello, Kyle."

To his credit, the boy looked him dead in the eyes. No frown, no smile, no hint of how furious he'd been earlier. "Hey."

Shifting his weight on shoes that probably cost

more than Ridge made in three months, Peter cleared his throat. "It's been a long time. Do you know who I am?"

"Sure. You're the reason I get to grow up in this awesome place."

The blow landed, and Ridge thought Peter might have actually taken a step back. He regained his composure quickly, though, and turned to Emily. "Hello, sweetheart."

Angelic blue eyes tilted up to study him, and she cocked her head. "My mommy says I shouldn't talk to strangers."

Marianne managed to take that one with a completely straight face, and Ridge was amazed. Hoping to help out a little, he stood and offered his hand. "Ridge Collins."

Unsmiling, Peter accepted the gesture. "Peter Weston."

"Nice to meet you, Pete."

Ridge kept his expression neutral, but he couldn't miss Marianne's quick grin. He didn't know why, but he loved to make this very serious woman smile.

"It's Peter," the man corrected him stiffly.

"Right. My bad."

"Can I ask what you're doing here?"

Peter cast a quick look at Kyle, and his unspoken message was clear. *What are you doing here with my son*?

But Kyle wasn't his—not even close—and Ridge's temper began to simmer. How dare this smooth-talking phony stroll into Marianne's kitchen and brush her aside? How dare he connect with his son and all but ignore his daughter? And then question the guy who'd been hanging out with them, playing games, helping with the team?

This suit had some serious nerve.

Ridge would like nothing more than to dress Peter Weston down, but it wasn't his place. "I'm a friend of Matt's, helping out with the farm. And you?"

The shocked look on Peter's tanning-booth face made Ridge want to laugh, but he managed to make it a smile instead.

"I'm here to see Kyle," Peter informed him coolly.

Not Emily, Ridge filled in easily enough. What was up with that? He wondered if Marianne knew. For now, he folded his arms, and they stared at each other for several seconds. He was dying to challenge Peter, but he knew it wouldn't go over well with Marianne. So he finally just nodded and sat down. It was the hardest thing he'd ever done, backing down from this pompous piece of work.

"You and Kyle can visit outside, if you want," Marianne offered.

Peter cast a nervous look at the dog framed in the screen door. "No, that's all right. The living room is fine. Would you like to join us, Emily?" he added, clearly an afterthought.

Tipping her head to assess her evolving picture, she didn't look at him, but very politely said, "No, thank you."

Ridge barely managed to strangle a laugh into a cough, and he swallowed some of Kyle's drink, hoping to make it look like he had something caught in his throat. He knew he wasn't fooling anybody, though, and Kyle grinned over at him before following his father into the living room.

Marianne, however, wasn't amused. "What is *wrong* with you?" she demanded, slapping him with a dish towel. "Are you twelve?"

"It was funny. Sue me." Grinning over at Emily, he winked. "Nice one, sweetness."

"Thank you. I don't like him," she added, wrinkling her cute button nose in distaste. "He's too fancy."

Ridge glanced through the arched doorway to find Peter on the couch and Kyle sitting in a wing-back chair on the other side of the living room. Apparently, Kyle shared his sister's opinion of their long-absent father.

Ridge turned slightly toward Marianne so he could whisper, "What's his problem with Emily?"

Marianne shrugged. "She's a girl."

"That's nuts."

"I know, but that's how it is." She sighed. "I wonder what he's up to."

"What makes you say that?"

"In all the time we've been here, he's only called Kyle a few times. I don't even know if he's still living in Chicago, and he's never asked to come see us. Why would he pick now?"

He didn't have an answer for that, but the barely disguised fear in Marianne's voice made his hackles go up like Tucker's. Reaching over, Ridge covered her hand with his and gave a reassuring squeeze. He wanted to tell her she wasn't in this alone, that he'd gladly step into that fight with her if she wanted him to. But knowing how deep her independent streak went, he suspected that any offer of help would only make her angry.

"Whatever it is," he said confidently, "you'll handle it."

Flashing him a quick smile, she slid her hand away. "Would you like some of that cherry pie?"

"Please."

As she got up, the worry lingering in her eyes made his gut twist with uncertainty. Unable to resist spying, Ridge looked into the living room again. Peter seemed to be doing most of the talking, trying to draw a very distrustful kid into some kind of conversation. Marianne's suspicions echoed in his mind, and right there he made a decision.

If Peter even hinted at making trouble for Marianne or her kids, he'd have to go through Ridge to do it.

Chapter Seven

After an hour that felt like forever, Peter finally said goodbye to Kyle and stood up. Marianne had been trying to give them some privacy, but they weren't that far away, and it was obvious the conversation was mostly one-sided. While she didn't wish for trouble between father and son, she had to be honest with herself. Watching Kyle give Peter the silent treatment told her she'd been right to bring her children home to Harland.

As Peter strolled toward the kitchen, she began clicking through the screens of her new online lesson. She'd already finished reading it, but she wanted to make it look as if she'd been busy with schoolwork instead of trying not to eavesdrop.

"He hates me." A baffled look creased Peter's perfectly chiseled features. "I don't understand it."

"You call twice a year and we have no idea where you live," Marianne reminded him without looking up from the monitor. "He doesn't even know you." Feeling brave, she lifted her head and looked him straight in the eyes. "I warned you."

She felt a little nudge on her ankle, and out of the corner of her eye she saw Ridge's mouth quirk approvingly. He was making a good show of building a log cabin and pony stable with Emily, but Marianne still caught the twinkle in his hazel eyes. It made her feel like a championship fighter who'd landed a solid punch on her opponent.

"I don't want it to be this way," Peter continued.

Clearly, he assumed she cared. She longed to tell him the truth but held back. If she started a fight with him, it would upset the kids. Besides, he was much meaner than she was. If she mounted a direct assault, he'd probably slaughter her.

"You can't just walk back into his life and expect him to accept you." The fact that he'd still barely glanced at his daughter broke Marianne's heart, but that was another problem. In all honesty, Emily was better off in her blissful little bubble.

"I need to get to know him, let him get to know me," Peter said, as though that was a novel idea.

For five years Marianne had been dreading the day he strolled back into their lives. Instinctively she'd known it would happen at some point. She prayed that Kyle was strong enough to handle it.

Even though she knew where this was headed, she asked, "What do you want?"

"The visits the judge gave me in court."

What about the child support he gave us? she wanted to snarl. But she didn't dare get into a serious legal argument with him. If she decided to go down that road, she'd have to think very carefully about how rough the trip would be. She'd end up with some much-needed funds, but at what cost?

Now that they were old enough to be consulted, a judge would want to talk to Kyle and Emily, get their input about seeing Peter. Marianne suspected that their comments about this stranger who happened to be their father wouldn't be flattering. In all likelihood, Peter's shark of a lawyer would spin that to make it Marianne's fault, and she'd have to prove otherwise. The fact that the shark was his brother meant Peter could fight her in court forever free of charge, while she went bankrupt paying someone to represent her and the kids. Just the thought of it horrified her.

Putting aside her misgivings in the interest of keeping the peace, she offered, "You can visit with him here, as long as I'm home."

Her ex-husband's mouth dropped open, his dark eyes snapping with the temper she knew was always coursing just beneath his debonair façade. "That's ridiculous."

"That's the deal," she shot back, glaring so he'd know she meant business. "Take it or leave it."

To her surprise, Peter rounded on Ridge. "This is your fault. You've turned her into a shrew."

At first, Ridge didn't even move. But watching him with her kids and the football team, she'd witnessed firsthand his fiercely protective nature. Marianne held her breath, silently pleading with him to restrain himself.

Very slowly he leaned back in his chair and folded his arms. His blue T-shirt flexed over the kind of hard-work muscles Peter didn't even know existed. Disdain and barely controlled fury raged in Ridge's eyes, at serious odds with his calm demeanor. He traded a long, very masculine look with her ex, and Marianne held her breath, wondering who would flinch first.

To her absolute delight, Peter ducked his head, brushing some nonexistent lint from his Armani jacket. "I'll be in touch."

Because she was a Southern lady, she escorted him to the door. Tucker still hadn't moved, and he growled his opinion of their unwelcome guest. Curbing a smile, she hooked his collar in her fingers so Peter could safely walk out to his car. As she watched him drive away, though, her amusement faded.

"What's wrong?" Ridge asked, suddenly right

behind her. She hadn't heard his footsteps, but she was glad to have him there. She didn't need it, but she liked knowing that he had her back.

"The license plate on his car," she replied, feeling deflated. "It's from D.C."

"So?"

Marianne turned to him, unable to believe that he couldn't piece it all together. Then again, he probably wasn't used to dealing with two-faced skunks like Peter. "That would be a little far to drive in a rental car, don't you think?"

After a second, it clicked, and he grimaced. "You think he's living in Washington now."

"I know he is."

"That's a long drive, even in a nice car like that. Why didn't he just fly?"

"He hates planes."

Ridge gave her a wry grin. "And I love 'em. Ironic, huh?"

"Very." She stared at the taillights as the luxurious car turned onto the highway. "He always wanted to be in D.C. All those powerbrokers and politicians really appealed to him."

"Bunch of corrupt peas in a pod." Ridge spat the words as if they tasted bitter in his mouth.

"Tell me about it."

"Yeah, that's the place for him, all right. Unfortunately, it's a lot closer than Chicago," he added in a tone that told her he understood the problem.

"It sure is." Marianne sent up a heartfelt prayer for strength. If Peter intended to stake some kind of claim to the family he'd abandoned, she'd need all the help she could get.

Bitter memories bubbled to the surface, and she couldn't resist saying, "I wonder if he brought his little redheaded cupcake with him."

"He cheated on you?" Ridge exploded, rage darkening his usually cheerful expression.

"With the neighbor's nanny. When she told me, I felt like I was the idiot wife in a really bad movie."

"You're not an idiot."

"It was a long time ago," she replied. "I've learned a lot since then."

"Like not to trust anybody with a Y chromosome."

Marianne took serious exception to that statement. "I don't mistrust men in general. I look at one person at a time. If they're trustworthy, I trust them. If not, I don't."

"Really? When's the last time you dated anyone?"

"You have no right to pry into my personal life," she retorted, glaring up at him. Already edgy from Peter's visit, she was aware that she was overreacting, but she couldn't seem to stop herself.

"Seriously? After all the time we've spent together, I can't believe you feel that way. But if you're still not convinced about me, I guess there's nothing I can do."

"There's nothing to do or not do. It's really none of your business."

The words had more snap to them than she'd intended, and Marianne recognized she was verbally pushing him away. Ridge's dark look vanished, replaced by an expression so devoid of emotion it startled her. He did nothing halfheartedly, and seeing that blank look on his face upset her more than if he'd yelled at her.

"Y'know, I've got a great life," he said quietly. "I don't need all this drama."

He was bailing on her, the way she'd feared all along. The way Peter had when things got rocky. She'd given Ridge an out, to see what he'd do, and he'd let her down.

Crushed, Marianne drew herself up with every ounce of dignity she'd inherited from generations of Sawyers who never let anything—or anyone— keep them down for long. "None of this is your responsibility. The farm and the team will get along just fine without you. You can leave whenever you want."

Because she didn't trust herself to say anything more without crying, she turned her back on him and went inside.

More furious than he'd been in a long time, Ridge stalked into the equipment barn and picked up a small sledgehammer from the tool rack. For lack of anything better to vent his frustration, he began pounding on the bent driveshaft from the most ancient of the Sawyers' old tractors. John took one look at him and wisely headed out with the newly repaired baler. Ridge made a mental note to apologize later. Right now he wasn't in the mood for company.

He'd done everything he could to prove himself to Marianne, he groused as he pounded on the metal bar. He'd been honest, understanding and patient to the nth degree. He was killing himself keeping his business going while helping with the farm and football. These weren't his fields, but he was working them for nothing. Football was a volunteer gig, too. Both ate up time he could have spent giving the aerial tours that were a huge moneymaker for him.

In spite of all his efforts, his bank account was just barely holding steady. Before long, it would go into free fall, and he hadn't made an inch worth of progress with Marianne. When it had seemed as if there might be a chance for something with her, he hadn't minded so much. Now he wasn't so sure.

Because he wasn't paying attention, the sledgehammer slipped and Ridge managed to bang his hand on the vise holding the driveshaft. Yelping, he lifted his bloody knuckles to his mouth and berated himself for being so careless. He found a reasonably clean kerchief and wrapped it around his fingers. While he tied the knot with his teeth, his eyes wandered out the open barn door.

Her blue-and-yellow fuselage glistening in the sun, Betsy beckoned to him, promising an escape from his dark mood. Figuring a quick flight would help him get things in perspective, Ridge put down the hammer and headed out to his pride and joy.

Inside three minutes, he was in the air.

Just lifting off the ground cleared his mind. After three months of being more or less grounded, the freedom felt incredible. As he soared over the gorgeous landscape, he admired the layout of farms surrounding the little town that had welcomed him with open arms. The Sawyer place was one of the biggest, and he felt a twinge of guilt when he noticed Matt and John snaking their way through their expansive new hayfield, baling and stacking.

From up here he could see how big the field was, and it looked like a daunting task. From their viewpoint, it must seem endless. The stacking job was the toughest, he knew from painful recent experience. Tomorrow he'd take John's place in the wagon and give his friend a break.

That he didn't even think of not going back made him chuckle. Something about Harland had drawn him in, refusing to let him go. He knew what—or rather who—that something was, but he forced his mind to clear so he could enjoy this time to himself. He used to have more of it than he knew what to do with. Now it was so rare, he wanted to savor it.

As he flew on, the tension gradually eased from his body, freeing him to focus on the thorniest problem he'd ever faced.

Marianne.

He wasn't one to trust people easily, so he understood being cautious. Even worse than he was, she didn't have faith in anyone outside her family and the Harland town limits. He wouldn't be surprised to learn that she didn't even trust herself anymore.

That was it, he suddenly realized. If Marianne didn't have faith in her own judgment, he could be a walking saint and she wouldn't follow her instincts. He'd been going about this all wrong. He didn't need to prove himself to her.

He had to convince her to trust herself again. The problem was, he had no clue where to start.

John or Matt might have a suggestion, but he hesitated to ask her brothers for advice like this. After mulling it over for a few seconds, he grinned and headed for the tiny Harland airport. He didn't need a Sawyer boy for this one.

He needed a Sawyer girl.

Ridge landed at the airstrip and strolled over to the only other person there.

"Hey, Gary," he greeted the easygoing mechanic. "By any chance, are you heading into town later on?"

Gary pulled an antique pocket watch from his bib overalls and checked the time. "About half an hour. I'm having supper with my folks, then coming back out here to finish up some maintenance in the hangar. You want a ride back?"

"That'd be great, thanks."

Because he had nothing else to do, Ridge grabbed a rag and started cleaning Gary's tools. Thirty minutes later, Gary left Ridge outside Ruthy's.

"See you around eight," he said before heading in the other direction.

Ridge waved and went inside, hoping to find Lisa. While he scanned the crowd looking for her, the owner noticed him at the counter and came over.

"Hello there," Ruthy greeted him with the bright

smile that seemed to be a permanent feature of her face. "What can I get you?"

"Nothing. I'm looking for Lisa."

"You just missed her. Is everything okay?"

"Yeah." Ridge sighed in frustration. "I had a question for her."

"About?" Ruthy cocked her head with a knowing look, and he laughed.

"All right, you got me. I need some advice about Marianne."

"I gave you some," she reminded him, eyes twinkling with humor. "Nuts and all."

"I know, but it's not working. I got the shell cracked open, but I'm hoping Lisa can help me get the nut out before it drives me over the edge."

Harland's favorite chef gave him a motherly smile, tinged with more than a little wisdom. "You're a good man, Ridge."

"Tell Marianne that, would you?" he pleaded while Ruthy scribbled down Lisa's address for him.

"I have." She handed over the slip of paper, adding an encouraging pat on his arm. "Don't give up on her. She'll come around."

"Thanks."

Taking Ridge's arm, she walked him to the door. Just before he left, he turned to her. "It's totally crazy, but I think I'm in love with her."

Ruthy laughed. "Oh, I know you're in love with

her. Now go talk to Lisa. Nobody knows that sister of hers better than she does."

Ridge left the diner and followed Ruthy's directions to a brick building a couple of blocks away. As he climbed the outside stairs that led to Lisa's apartment, he heard a sound that fell somewhere between a growl and a moan.

Looking up, he saw what looked like a miniature lynx sprawled out in a garden window filled with flowers and framed by lacy curtains. It watched him through the screen with eerie gold eyes, as if it were tracking his every step. When Ridge got to the landing, the cat opened its large mouth and howled. If it hadn't been on the other side of the window, Ridge would definitely have taken a step back.

He'd gotten used to the shamelessly friendly Tucker. This cat gave him the creeps.

On the door hung a wreath made from an assortment of dried flowers, and in the middle was an old brass knocker. The sharp crack of it on the wood spooked the cat, and it vanished from its perch as if it had never been there. Weird.

When Lisa opened the door and saw it was him, she frowned. "What's wrong?"

"Nothing. Why would you think something's wrong?"

She just stared up at him. After a few seconds,

he caved. "Okay. I need some advice. About Marianne," he added to be absolutely clear.

"Well, duh." Closing the door behind her, she motioned him to a bistro table and chairs farther down the second-story deck. "Cleo's not crazy about people besides me, so we should stay out here."

"Cleo?"

"As in Cleopatra," she explained with a grin. "She thinks she's the queen of the universe."

They sat down, and even though he'd come here for her help, Ridge realized that he had no idea what to say. "That's one big cat."

"I found her by the road when she was a kitten. She was pretty sick, but she managed to fight her way back."

"So you named her after Cleopatra. Cool."

They traded awkward small talk for a few minutes. Finally, Lisa sat back in her chair and folded her arms the way her brothers did when they were serious. "So, what's up?"

"Peter came by the farm earlier."

"I know. I saw him at the diner, and when I called later, Marianne told me he was going to the farm. I wanted to be there, but she said she had it handled. Stubborn," she added, shaking her head in disapproval. "But that's my big sister. Always the strong one."

"Yeah, that's probably why she questioned what kind of man I was," he continued, feeling his temper spike. "I just about lost it, so I ended up out in the barn. Even John wouldn't talk to me."

Lisa laughed. "It takes a lot to get through to him. I can only imagine how mad you looked."

Leaning in, Ridge confided, "She's driving me crazy."

Lisa tilted her head with a very feminine smirk. "In a good way or a bad way?"

"Both." Throwing himself back in his chair, he scowled at no one in particular. "What do I do about it?"

"What do you want to do about it?"

"You sound like Ruthy."

She beamed her approval. "What a fabulous compliment. Thank you."

At first, he was baffled by the response. Then he realized he'd subconsciously meant the dig in a positive way, and he laughed. His latest wrangle with Marianne was really messing with his sense of humor. "You're welcome. Any suggestions?"

To his dismay, she shook her head. "Thanks to the spineless weasel who shall remain nameless, Marianne's as skittish as they come. If you've got your heart set on her, you'll have to be patient."

"Great."

"On the plus side," Lisa went on as if he hadn't

spoken, "you're the kind of guy she needs. She thinks she wants some educated, suave business-man who can talk about art and books with her. What she needs is a strong, dependable guy who will love her and the kids and do anything he can to make them happy."

While Ridge absorbed that tidbit, something she'd said jumped out at him. "Books?"

"She loves to read, especially the classics. Her favorite is *Little Women*."

"Really? I was in her office and saw all those books. How come she doesn't have a copy of it?"

"Dad got her a first edition as a college gradu-ation gift. It came in two volumes, and they got ruined when she moved to Chicago. One of the klutzes unpacking her stuff sliced through the bindings with a utility knife, and the books fell apart."

The revelation dinged a bell in the back of Ridge's mind. The books were like Marianne, whole and solid when they were in Harland, de-stroyed when she left home. Ridge wasn't big on possessions himself, and he'd gotten the impres-sion Marianne wasn't all that materialistic, either. But losing the present her father had given her on such an important occasion must have been dev-astating.

Now that Ethan was gone, Ridge instinctively

knew that regaining those prized books would make Marianne feel more connected to the life she'd had before she lost her footing with Peter.

Suddenly inspired, he jumped to his feet. "Thanks, Lisa. You just gave me a great idea."

As he raced past her and down the steps, Cleopatra unleashed a parting howl while Lisa called after him, "What idea?"

Too excited to stop, he waved and all but ran back to Ruthy's Place so he could use a landline. He knew someone who could help him prove to Marianne just what kind of man he was. But the elderly gentleman lived in London, and it was getting close to his bedtime.

The next morning, Ridge still hadn't come back.

He'd told her he couldn't legally fly Betsy at night. Once it had gotten dark, Marianne knew he wouldn't return until the following day. If he decided to come back at all.

So she'd tossed and turned all night, unable to put their argument out of her mind. She felt awful for chasing him off, but she didn't know what to do about it. His question about her dating wasn't anything she hadn't heard before, but she'd retaliated in a way that was utterly unlike her. She could have blamed it on the strain Peter's visit caused her, but she knew perfectly well that was a cop-out.

Ridge made her feel things she hadn't felt in a long time, emotions she wasn't prepared to deal with. Rather than embrace them and see where they might lead, she'd pushed them—and him—away. She was trying to protect herself, but even she recognized that that was a flimsy excuse.

In reality, she'd been trying not to get attached to the charismatic pilot who'd landed in her life. Sighing, she had to admit that she'd failed completely. He'd nudged under her defenses the first time she met him, and she'd been fighting a losing battle ever since.

Now he was gone, and it was all her fault.

Kyle jumped down the last few steps into the kitchen, yanking her out of her funk.

"Where's Ridge?" he asked.

"I'm not sure," she replied, trying to sound unconcerned. "Would you like pancakes or waffles?"

"Pancakes, please." He glanced out the window to the empty spot where Betsy usually sat. "When's he coming back?"

"I don't know."

I don't even know if *he's coming back,* she added silently while she ladled batter onto the griddle.

Kyle eyed her suspiciously. "Did you two have a fight?"

"No." He cocked his head in disbelief, and she amended her answer. "Well, sort of. More of a misunderstanding than a fight."

"Like you and my father used to have?"

She'd worked so hard to keep their arguments from Kyle, it just about killed her to know he'd heard them. And remembered them. Taking a deep breath to steady her voice, she carefully wiped down the batter bowl and set it on the counter. "You heard us?"

Kyle nodded. "You always let him win. Ridge says you should never give up and let anybody beat you."

She knew Ridge attached a double meaning to those words, and she appreciated him sharing that very important lesson with her son.

"I didn't realize you knew so much back then," she admitted while she flipped his pancakes.

"You did your best, Mom. Nobody can do any more than that."

Recognizing another of Ridge's sayings, Marianne smiled. "Thanks, bud. I'll try to remember that."

As he poured himself some orange juice, Kyle said, "If you apologize, Ridge'll forgive you. He's cool like that."

Marianne just hoped she'd get the chance to

follow his advice. Fortunately, Emily bounced in to distract her.

"Waffles, please!" her daughter sang, plunking herself down beside Kyle.

As she switched over to start a batch of waffles, Marianne found herself listening for the now-familiar rumble of Betsy's engine. When she heard it faintly, she wondered if it was her imagination. As it grew louder, she blew out a tense breath.

Thank you, God, for bringing him back.

Tucker loped out to greet Ridge, and he gave the Lab some love before heading inside. He was wearing the same clothes he'd left in, and judging by their rumpled look, he'd slept in them.

When he came up the back steps and into the kitchen, her apology stuck in her throat. She was so insanely happy to see him, she literally couldn't form any coherent words.

"Morning, everybody," he said casually, dropping into a chair across from the kids. "What's up?"

"We're going to the zoo today," Emily informed him happily.

"Wanna come with us?" Kyle asked.

"That depends. They have any chimps at this zoo?"

"Tons," Kyle assured him. "Gorillas, too."

"And howler monkeys," Emily chimed in. "They're so funny."

Ridge grinned at her. "Why's that?"

"They go like this." And she proceeded to give an alarmingly good imitation of their high-pitched screech.

Chuckling, Ridge glanced over at Marianne. He gave her a questioning look, as if he were asking her permission to join them. That was when she realized that she should have been the one to invite him.

"We'd love to have you come along if you're not too busy," she said.

"I thought I'd give Matt and John a hand today, but if you can wait till this afternoon, I'm game."

"Are you sure?" Marianne asked. "You look like you slept in Betsy's cockpit."

"Actually, Gary let me crash on the sofa in his office at the airstrip." He twisted his back from side to side. "I think it's older than I am—it was a little lumpy."

As if she didn't feel bad enough already. Her regret must have shown on her face, because Ridge fixed her with one of those direct gazes that made her heart trip over itself.

"I'm fine, Marianne." After an intense moment, his eyes lightened, and he grinned. "I wouldn't mind some of those waffles, though."

She was forgiven. Thrilled beyond belief, Marianne filled a mug with coffee for him. Setting it on the table, she patted his shoulder and gave him a grateful smile. She pulled away, but Ridge surprised her by resting his hand over hers.

When her eyes met his, the look he gave her warmed her right down to her toes. Before she could think of something to say, he lifted her hand and brushed a kiss over the back. With a gentle squeeze, he finally let it go, and it fell limply to her side.

With her brain completely frozen, she could only stare at him. The sweet, romantic gesture was so unlike him, she was at a complete loss for words.

"Mommy, are you okay?"

Emily's voice dragged her back to reality, and Marianne stammered, "I'm fine."

"You're kinda red," Kyle noticed, cocking his head in confusion. "You sure you're okay?"

"Absolutely." Putting some distance between herself and Ridge seemed like a smart move right now, and she tried to look casual about it. Judging by the very male smirk on his face, she hadn't quite managed it.

She hadn't had that kind of reaction to a man in so long, she wasn't sure what to do about it. Turning away in embarrassment, she said, "Waffles coming up."

* * *

Ridge couldn't remember the last time he'd been to a zoo. He'd been on safaris, he'd even gone on a caribou hunt in Alaska that netted him some great pictures—but no caribou. They were faster than people thought.

But this, he decided after about five minutes, was more fun than all the exotic reserves he'd ever visited.

"Oh, I love the penguins," Emily cooed outside their rocky habitat. "The babies are so cute when they waddle around."

"He looks like Pastor Charles," Kyle commented, pointing to a pudgy one with a tuft of white feathers circling his head.

Marianne pointed to one who seemed to be gathering the younger ones together and leading them to the fish their keeper had just dropped in for them. "Who does that remind you of?"

"Ruthy!" they shouted together, and she smiled.

That was why he hadn't given up on her, Ridge realized with a clarity that stunned him. It was that smile, the one that lit up her entire face and sparkled in her eyes. In the three months he'd known her, he'd seen it maybe half a dozen times.

Marianne was a challenge. But she just might be worth it.

When had he decided that? he wondered as they

moved on to the polar bear section of the zoo. His feelings for Marianne had snuck up on him when he wasn't looking, which didn't make him feel any better about them. Taking her hand for a kiss was definitely not his style, and he frowned at the memory. Instinct—or insanity?

Probably a little of both, he admitted with a sigh.

As the kids ran ahead, he and Marianne lagged behind. This was his chance to prove to himself that the old-fashioned gesture had just been a momentary lapse. He was pretty tired, after all. So he reached down and gently took her hand, holding it loosely enough that she could pull away if she wanted.

She didn't.

Panic seized in his chest, and Ridge racked his brain for a polite way to let go without hurting her feelings. Then, to his surprise, she wove her fingers through his and leaned into his shoulder a little.

Toward him, he realized. Reaching out to him, not pushing him away. It felt as if she was giving him room the way he'd done with her, but he wanted to get closer. It might not be the smartest thing to do, but he couldn't help it. As he slipped an arm around her shoulders, she cuddled in closer, resting her head on his chest.

It felt amazing.

By the time they reached the polar bears' lake house, Ridge knew that despite all his efforts to keep his distance, he'd fallen in love with her. He wasn't sure how he felt about that, but the barking of sea lions broke into his thoughts and dragged him back into the moment.

The sea lions chased each other through the water, plopping up onto rocks to wave at their visitors and pose for pictures. They barked for attention, and people laughed, pointing out different animals to their kids.

One of them splashed water toward the kids, and Emily squealed in delight. "He wants to play with us!"

"Let's go downstairs and watch them swim," Marianne suggested, holding a hand out for Emily.

Kyle was eyeing him with curiosity, and Ridge realized he still had his arm around Marianne. Hoping he looked cool, he did the bro-hug thing with her son, and they started walking.

"It's okay," Kyle whispered, grinning up at him.

Ridge chuckled quietly. "Thanks."

The girls headed down the rocky steps ahead of them, and Kyle added, "She smiles a lot more when you're around."

"Really?" Ridge's heart swelled with pride. "That's good to know."

A huge expanse of glass showed visitors what the sea lions looked like underwater. They darted through arches and playfully skimmed past each other, making sure they swam close to the people standing there watching them.

As the four of them clustered near the viewing glass, Ridge noticed Emily jumping up trying to see better.

"Here, sweetness," he said, lifting her to sit on his shoulders. "This'll help."

"Thank you, Ridge," she said very politely. "This is much better."

"Glad I could help."

"Look at us, Mommy," she went on. "We're like a real family today."

"We're always a real family," Kyle corrected her sharply.

"Of course we are." Marianne smoothed his temper with an understanding smile. "But it's nice to have Ridge with us, don't you think?"

The poor kid looked down and kicked his sneaker on the mosaic of a snowy mountain range. "Yeah." Lifting his head, he frowned up at Ridge. "Sorry."

"For what? You've got a great family, and I'm just happy to be here with you guys."

Nudging Kyle's shoulder, Ridge grinned and got a grateful look in return. Every instinct he had was screaming at him to back off and quit digging this hole he'd gotten himself into. But deep inside him, a quieter voice urged him to let go of his past failures and open himself up for something better.

The love and sense of belonging he'd spent years searching for was within his grasp. All he had to do was put aside his fear and hold on to it.

Their trip to the zoo was fun but exhausting, and about ten minutes into the ride home, both kids were sound asleep in the backseat.

After checking on them, Marianne turned back around and smiled at Ridge. He'd offered to drive home, and she'd gladly agreed. "They had a great time. Thanks so much for coming with us."

"It was good for me, too," he assured her as he steered onto the highway. "Can't remember the last time I had that much fun."

"I hope you won't be too far behind in your work."

Glancing over, he gave her the confident grin she'd admired the first time she saw him. "I'll just be at it a little longer tomorrow. It's a good trade for being with all of you today."

"Peter never went anywhere with us unless I begged."

As soon as the words left her mouth, Marianne wished she could snatch them back. Why on earth had she confided something like that to Ridge? She must sound like an old harpy.

To her amazement, he pulled the van onto the shoulder of the highway and put it in Park. After glancing into the backseat, he shifted to face her.

Taking both of her hands, he looked at her with the most serious expression she'd ever seen from him. "I'm not like Peter."

He didn't sound angry, but his tone was very firm, like he was trying to convince her of something she didn't want to believe. "I know that."

"Do you?" Cocking his head, his eyes bored into hers with an intensity that surprised her. "Because sometimes I feel like you're just waiting for me to screw up so you'll have an excuse not to like me."

Oh, it was way too late for that, Marianne lamented silently. She liked this fun-loving pilot more than she should, and it wouldn't take much to nudge her completely over the edge. Reason asserted itself, though, reminding her that this man had taken off when things between them got heated, just as Peter used to.

Pulling her hands free, she folded them tightly to keep Ridge from touching her. "Why did you leave like that yesterday?"

He shrugged as if it were nothing. "I was mad. I needed time to think about things."

"Like?"

"Like you," he muttered. Rubbing his hands over his face, he gave her a wry grin. "You drive me crazy."

"You drive me crazy, too," she assured him sternly, "but I don't take off without telling you where I'm going."

He opened his mouth, then closed it and shook his head. "Got me there." A smile worked its way across his tanned features, and he added, "I'm sorry."

Marianne wanted to retaliate, tell him it was too late for apologies. Instead, she heard herself say, "I was up all night worrying."

Interest warmed the gold in his eyes, and he edged toward her. "Really?"

"You could crash, or Betsy might have engine trouble and strand you somewhere." Even to her, that sounded hollow, and she had to smile. "I'd hate it if anything happened to you."

"Trust me, so would I. I think God grounded me in Harland for a reason, and I'd hate to miss anything He has in mind for me."

Cradling her cheek in his hand, he leaned in and brushed a kiss over her lips. It felt as if he were gently asking her a question, and Marianne was only too happy to answer it.

Returning that kiss was the most natural thing

she'd ever done. As the kiss deepened, something inside her rustled as if it had awakened from a long sleep and was happy to be coaxed back to life.

Ridge broke the kiss, resting his forehead on hers with a sigh. "You know the kids are watching us, right?"

"Yes."

Smiling because she simply couldn't help herself, she leaned in and kissed him again.

Chapter Eight

"I don't wanna get to know my father," Kyle protested, his normally calm demeanor rigid and determined. As he sat at the picnic table under a tree, his attitude was at odds with the peaceful setting. "He was mean to you and Emily the other day, and I don't ever wanna see him again."

He completely ignored the snack Marianne had prepared to help ease what she'd known would be a tense conversation. Sitting back on the picnic table bench, he glowered at her, folding his arms to prove he meant business. She had never seen him do that, and it brought home just how quickly he was growing up. In that pose, he reminded her of someone, and it took less than a second to recognize who.

Ridge.

Thinking of the fun-loving pilot stirred up emotions she'd rather not acknowledge while her belligerent son sat across from her, glaring for all he was worth. Marianne pushed Ridge from her mind and focused on the problem at hand.

"You have every right to feel that way," she began, stopping abruptly when he let out an impatient sigh. "What?"

"You sound like the school psychologist. I'm not crazy."

"Of course not, honey."

His look darkened at what he considered a babyish endearment, and she hurried on. "Kyle, I'll be honest with you. I don't know how to handle this. The law says your father has a right to see you, and I have to abide by that."

"Don't I have a right *not* to see him?"

"Sure you do," Ridge chimed in from behind her. "But if you do that, he'll blame your mom for interfering. Is that what you want?"

Marianne angled an irritated look at Ridge. "This is a private discussion."

Clearly unfazed, he plunked himself down in a lawn chair at the head of the table, folding his arms on the weathered planks in front of him. Focused entirely on Kyle, he said, "I'm gonna tell you a story I don't tell many people. I want you to listen, and when I'm done, I'll leave you alone. Deal?"

Without a flicker of hesitation, Kyle nodded.

That unthinking gesture told Marianne just how much her son had come to trust this man.

"I know a little something about father trouble," Ridge began.

"You never talk about your dad," Kyle commented. "How come?"

Ridge's jaw tightened, and he made an obvious effort to relax. "My father was a mean drunk, and he drank every day."

His voice sounded flat and dead. This part of his life was long ago, but she could see that talking about it still made him furious. She suspected that his only defense was to keep a firm grip on those memories so they couldn't get loose and hurt him anymore. Unfortunately, she'd handled the demise of her marriage the same way, so she understood all too well.

"The night of my fourteenth birthday," Ridge continued, "he started in on me, and my mom stepped in to protect me. When he went after her, I put him in the hospital for a week."

Hesitance flashed in his eyes as he glanced at Marianne, and she read the plea in them as clearly as if he'd spoken it out loud.

Please don't hate me.

She couldn't imagine how many years it had taken that angry, bitter young man to come to terms with the abuse he and his mother had suffered and move past it. Somehow, through the grace of God, he'd grown into the kind, caring man who was sitting at a picnic table baring his soul to her and her son. Not for his own benefit, but to help them with a problem that wasn't his concern. Reliving those memories couldn't be easy for him, and his selflessness amazed her.

Not usually one for retribution, she rested a hand over his. "It sounds like he got what he deserved."

Gratitude flooded Ridge's eyes, and he gently grasped her hand before turning back to Kyle. "When school was out, we came to North Carolina to live with Mom's cousin."

"To keep you away from your father," Marianne guessed.

Ridge nodded. "After I graduated, we went back to Denver because she missed her parents. When my father died in a car accident, I knew she'd be safe from him, so I left."

Kyle met Marianne's gaze with a hardness she'd never seen. "Did my father do that to you?"

"No," she assured him quickly. "This is Ridge's story, not ours."

Still holding Marianne's hand, he rested the other one on Kyle's shoulder. "I didn't mean to scare you, but I wanted you to know I get it. It's tough to be around someone who can hurt you and the people you care about."

"Kyle." Marianne waited for him to look at her. "I promise you don't have to be alone with your father if you don't want to. I'll be here, or Uncle John or Ridge."

Her motherly instinct urged her to forbid the visits completely, but she realized that would only anger Peter, and he might end up taking her to court to enforce his rights. While she didn't like the idea of his invading her home, she could manage it.

Her concern was that if Peter chose to take her to court, Kyle would be dragged into some judge's chambers to answer a lot of uncomfortable questions about the father he barely knew. As mature as he seemed, he was still only ten. If she could spare him that, she would. She hoped that, in time, Peter would tire of driving to North Carolina and would stay in D.C. with the other sharks.

To her great relief, Kyle smiled, once again her generous, easygoing boy. "Okay, Mom. I'll give it a shot."

She could hardly believe her ears. Apparently she could add magician to Ridge's eclectic résumé. "Are you sure?"

"Yeah, it'll be fine." Swinging up from the

bench, he whistled for his dog. "Me and Tucker are going for a run. Okay?"

Marianne was so proud of him, she didn't even bother to correct his grammar. "Sure. Come back before dark, though."

"We will."

The Lab barreled in from wherever he'd been roaming, and the two of them headed to the shed where Kyle kept his mountain bike. Watching them fly down the nearest field road, she smiled and then turned to Ridge.

"That can't have been easy for you," she said. "Thank you."

"Glad I could help." Stifling a yawn, he groaned. "All this football is killing me. I can't keep up with those kids."

Laughing, Marianne reached into the cooler beside the table and fished out a half-frozen water bottle for him. "I warned you."

Cracking open the bottle, he poured icy water into his mouth. "It's my own fault. I always leap before I look."

In truth, she liked that about him. So many people were cautious to the point of paralysis, watching the world spin around them with no idea how to join in. If she was completely honest, lately she'd begun to think she was one of those people.

She didn't make changes unless she was forced

to, like with her masters course on child devel-
opment that she was enjoying so much. The
revelation didn't thrill her, but Ridge's embrace-
everything philosophy had made her take a good,
long look at herself.

"Ridge, may I ask you something?"

Shifting, he slung an arm over his bent knee
and gave her one of his charmingly crooked grins.
"Sure."

"If you could change something about yourself,
what would it be?"

"I'd be smarter," he replied instantly.

"Come on. I'm serious."

"So am I."

"You're one of the smartest people I've ever
met." He gave her a doubtful look, and she added,
"Really. I didn't think so at first, but you are."

His grin widened, and she felt her face getting
hotter than the air around her. "What I meant
was—"

"I don't come across as well educated and
shrewd." He winked before swallowing some
water. "I'll take that as a compliment."

"That's not it, exactly." She tried to explain,
searching for the right words. "You're smart, but
you don't hold it over people. You've had a really interesting life, but instead of going on and
on about yourself, you focus on the person you're

talking to. You make them feel that you're interested in what they have to say."

He'd been watching her while they chatted, but his demeanor suddenly shifted. He didn't move closer, but his gaze locked with hers and, try as she would, she couldn't look away. The gold in his eyes warmed, making the green look even more vivid than usual.

"I'm interested, Marianne," he murmured, his voice filled with something she couldn't begin to define. "You can count on that."

When she heard gravel crunching in the driveway, she angled a look over her shoulder. Peter's silver Jag pulled in and parked next to her van. Wonderful.

As he strolled over, she stood to greet him. He looked down on her in every figurative way possible. She didn't want him doing it literally, too.

The fact that she didn't mind Ridge standing over her flashed into her mind. Pushing that thought away, she braced herself for another confrontation with her arrogant ex-husband.

"Marianne." Completely ignoring Ridge, Peter acknowledged her with a curt nod and looked past her toward the field road where Kyle was racing Tucker. "How's my boy doing?"

"Fine."

Peter's condescending tone brought back a flood

of memories she'd thought were dead and buried. She didn't want him anywhere near her or her children. Standing in her yard in his Italian suit and shoes, he stuck out like a peacock in a henhouse.

"If you'll excuse me," Ridge said as he stood, "I've got some work to do. Nice seeing you again, Pete."

"Peter," he said to Ridge's back. Sauntering past him and into the barn, the pilot didn't respond, but Marianne could imagine him grinning.

Hiding a smile of her own, she made an attempt at being civil. "Would you like something to drink, Peter?"

Intent on scowling at Ridge, he didn't seem to notice she'd said anything. Finally he looked at her. "What?"

She repeated her question, and he replied, "Iced tea would be nice."

Out of habit, she reached toward the ice chest to get it for him. But something stopped her. A murmur in the back of her mind reminded her that this man was no longer her husband. Not only that, he'd proven himself many times to be the enemy. Even the most old-fashioned Southern lady wasn't expected to serve the enemy.

Stepping back, she gave him access to the cooler. "Help yourself."

When he finally looked at her, the shock she saw

in his angular features was priceless. He opened the lid and reached inside to rummage through the assortment of bottles. Pulling out one labeled Sweet Tea, he frowned but twisted it open.

"I keep forgetting the Southern fondness for sweetening everything to death," he complained. "The dentists down here must make a real killing."

Because she had no desire to spar with him, Marianne let the snide comment go. She was dying to ask him how long he'd been living in Washington, but she cautioned herself against showing interest in anything he did. He'd neglected her and the kids for years. She refused to give him the satisfaction of appearing to care.

Her phone dinged from the picnic table, telling her she had a text. She wasn't surprised to see Ridge's name on the screen. When she opened the message, she couldn't help smiling: is that yutz bothrng u?

She glanced through the open door of the barn, but he was doing a good job appearing to be concentrating on something clamped into a vise on the workbench. She smiled at his inventive way of communicating with her. Ridge knew Peter didn't like the idea of them together, but he wanted Marianne to know he was watching out for her.

So she replied, fine here, adding a smiley wink so he'd know she really was okay.

Shifting his head, he angled a look back at her while he loosened a bolt with a wrench. She almost waved at him, but felt Peter watching her intently. So she kept up the ruse and texted, really.

Turning around, Ridge shook his head, and even from this distance she could tell he was debating whether to come over and see for himself. How could she ever have considered him selfish and irresponsible? Not only did it feel as if she'd made that judgment a very long time ago, it seemed impossible. As she had after Peter's first visit to the farm, she got a warm, comforting feeling knowing that if she needed him, Ridge was there.

It gave her confidence a nice boost, and she turned her attention back to Peter. His concentration was completely fixed on Kyle, smiling as he cleared a low jump with a flourish in the air. "That's my boy."

That he had the gall to claim anything as far as Kyle was concerned made Marianne's temper simmer. Rather than get angry, though, she decided to take the high road. Sort of.

"He and Ridge built that ramp," she commented lightly. "They're having fun with football, too. After practice, they come home and run more plays till it's too dark to see."

Mention of their semi-permanent guest had just the effect she'd anticipated. Peter's gaze left the field and landed squarely on her. There was a time when such intense contact with him had made her fidget, wondering what she'd done wrong. Now it just made her smile.

Her heart soared as it dawned on her that she wasn't afraid of him anymore.

"I'd rather you didn't flaunt your boyfriend in front of Kyle," Peter snarled. "He has a father."

She almost told him Ridge wasn't her boyfriend, but something made her hold back. The idea that she had someone in her life seemed to aggravate him, and she was enjoying his reaction.

"Fathers do more than conceive a child. They certainly don't leave them a note and never look back."

"Our circumstances had become untenable."

"Hauling out the big words now, are we?" she taunted, which was very unlike her.

Years of pent-up anger bubbled dangerously close to a boiling point, and she struggled to keep her composure. Peter wanted to upset her because that would give him a cool, logical advantage over her. She knew that letting him rile her would only play into that, but she'd had enough of his upper-crust attitude. He was on her turf. She didn't have to take any nonsense from him.

"I know perfectly well what they mean, you

know," she continued. "You're only half as smart as you think you are."

His eyes became dark slits, and she knew she'd pushed him too far. Old fears curled around her, and she fought the urge to take a step back. Those days were gone, she reminded herself.

She would never give ground to Peter Weston again.

"You used to be so sweet and accommodating." His silky voice did little to disguise the malicious current running beneath his words. "What happened to the girl I married?"

"She grew up." Raising her chin defiantly, Marianne glared at him. "With two children to raise, she didn't have a choice."

After a pause, Peter smirked. "I know Emily isn't mine."

Several unspeakable things popped into her mind. Somehow she managed to keep them to herself.

"She most certainly is," Marianne hissed. "Whatever problems we might have had, I was always faithful to you." Narrowing her eyes, she summoned all the humiliation he'd put her through during their marriage. "It's too bad you can't say the same."

From the astonishment on his face, she knew she'd hit the mark with that one. Peter thought she was a simple, foolish country girl so in love with him she couldn't see his flaws. It gave her great satisfaction to prove just how wrong he was about her.

After several moments, he apparently gave up trying to come up with a response. "I have a meeting elsewhere. Tell Kyle I'll see him tomorrow."

"Tomorrow isn't good. He gets home from school at three o'clock, and he does homework until we leave for practice at five."

Peter obviously had no clue school was even in session. Why would he? People without children didn't follow academic schedules, much less plan ahead for homework and playtime.

"Fine. I'll come Wednesday around four."

She hadn't invited him to come back, and his arrogant assumption galled her. Even though she knew immediately the time fit into their schedule, she made a show of thinking it over. "That's fine."

Peter walked away, then turned back. "For the record, Marianne, I don't like the changes I see in you. You've become bitter and manipulative, and I'm concerned that you're a bad influence on my son."

"Tell it to the judge."

He scowled his opinion of that. "I just might."

"Go right ahead," she shot back. "I have a few things to tell him myself."

That set Peter back on his heels, but only for a moment. Marianne savored the brief victory, but decided it was best to let the subject drop. After they glared at each other for what felt like a very long time, Peter finally retreated to his car.

The sound of gravel dinging the glossy finish on his Jag as he drove away was one of the nicest things Marianne had ever heard.

After a late supper, the kids were still wired. Ridge was afraid one of them might actually get hurt. Hoping to avoid a trip to the hospital, he suggested, "How 'bout a swim?"

Whooping their approval, they bounded upstairs to change into their suits. While they were gone, he grinned across the table at Marianne. "Gonna tell me why you look like a cat in cream?"

"Do I?" she asked, standing to start clearing the dishes. "I didn't realize."

"What did Petey want?"

He'd used the childish nickname to make her smile, and it worked. "To mark his territory. Unfortunately for him, Kyle isn't his to claim."

While she seemed fine to him, Ridge's back went up anytime he even thought of her ex being around her or the kids. Ridge had met a few men like Peter in his travels. Rich and arrogant, they assumed everything—and everyone—they saw was theirs for the taking. Trouble was, they didn't consider the fact that some folks didn't want to be taken.

"What did he say exactly?" Ridge pressed. He had a golden gut, and it was telling him there was trouble ahead somewhere.

Shrugging, she began loading the dishwasher. "He said he didn't like the changes he saw in me, that I was a bad influence on his son. He threatened to tell the judge, and I told him to go ahead because I have some things to tell the judge myself."

"Whoa!" Hands up, Ridge flung himself back in his chair, exaggerating his astonishment but not by much. "Nice one."

"I thought so."

She was still smiling when the kids barreled down the stairs and out the side door. As he followed Marianne outside, Ridge said, "That can't have been easy to do. You should be real proud of yourself."

"You know, I am." As Tucker and the kids simultaneously hit the water, she laughed. "He looked like he'd been kicked in a very bad place. You would've loved it."

"Wish I'd been there," he said lightly, hoping she'd get his real meaning.

Her grateful look told him she'd heard him loud and clear. "That's sweet, but I really was fine."

"I'm glad."

And proud, he added silently. He'd never been prouder of anyone in his life. How she'd gone from the trembling woman he'd seen during Peter's first visit to this growling mama bear was beyond him. He was just glad she'd made the leap. Things could only improve from here.

"Peter didn't stay long after that, but he'll be here Wednesday at four. That was the best I could do," she insisted, clearly anticipating his objection. "The law says he has a right to see his children, and I won't go against that."

Her mention of *children* got Ridge's temper going again. "How can he ignore Emily the way he does?"

"I'm not sure. But I think he'll get tired of Kyle's attitude before long, and our lives will go back to normal."

Except for mine, he thought as Emily shouted, "Watch me, Ridge!"

Watching her swim the width of the small pond, it occurred to him that he'd really come to care about this little family. It was uncharacteristic of him, and totally unexpected. The past few years he'd drifted wherever the wind took him, enjoying things as they came without becoming too attached to any place or anyone in particular. It worked for him, and he enjoyed his life. But sitting on the dock next to Marianne, watching Kyle and Emily play water tag with Tucker, he knew.

He didn't want to leave.

In his shorts pocket, his cell phone buzzed. He pulled it out and checked the caller I.D. When he saw it was Matt, he clicked the on button. "What's up?"

"There's a package here for you." His old friend chuckled. "It came earlier, but Caty just found it in a rosebush. The delivery guy must've set it on the porch railing and it fell into the garden."

Ridge's heart lurched, and he tried to sound normal. "Is it damaged?"

"Nah. It's a hard-sided case coated in plastic. Could probably survive being shot out of a cannon. What is it, anyway?"

"Just some books I ordered."

"From England?" Matt sounded suspicious. "Shakespeare's journals or something?"

"Something like that." He checked his watch and saw that it was nearly eight. "I know you go to bed early, so I'll come get it now."

"Don't bother. We'll keep it here for you."

Ridge repeated his plan, and he could hear Matt's shrug over the phone. "Suit yourself."

"See you in ten."

Marianne was eyeing him strangely. "You're going to Matt and Caty's now? Those must be some important books."

"They are," he said as he stood up. "I won't be long."

"Okay."

She looked bewildered, and he briefly wondered if she still thought he was crazy. Then again, he mused as he strolled toward the barn, he hadn't done anything just now to make her think otherwise.

Sighing to himself, he kicked Matt's bike to life and took off for town. Harland wasn't exactly a thriving metropolis during the day, but at night it looked downright sleepy. Even Ruthy's, which kept the longest hours of any small-town diner he'd ever seen, was closed. As he drove by, he saw lights on in the back kitchen windows and wondered what new culinary invention Ruthy was concocting back there. Whatever it was, he couldn't wait to taste it.

The monument in the square was lit by a single spotlight, giving it a ghostly appearance. The four churches surrounding it were dark except for a single electric candle in each window. With a crescent moon and twinkling stars overhead, it all seemed completely perfect to him.

Turning onto Oak Street, he saw the construction trailer still parked at the curb in front of the Sawyers' house. The structure was completely finished, the pale green siding all in place. As he shut down the bike, he saw Matt and Caty on the front porch swing. As he got closer, he heard them arguing.

"Leather's the way to go," Matt said, pointing to something in a catalog.

"Sure, if you like sticking to it when you get up," Caty scoffed. "I like this nice, cushy one."

Matt groaned, then noticed Ridge on the steps. "Help me out here, would ya?"

Ridge laughed. "Not a chance. I'm divorced for a reason."

"Would you like some lemonade?" Caty asked, motioning to a frosty pitcher on the little table. "I made it just a little while ago."

"Sounds great."

Ridge reached for an empty glass, but she shooed his hand away. "Sit down and let me do this."

"Yes, ma'am."

As he sat in a white wicker chair, she gave Matt a cheeky grin. "See? It's not that hard."

"Don't push it, sweetheart." He scowled at her, but the fond twinkle in his eyes betrayed him. Matt Sawyer, the wildest of the wild, had been tamed by a green-eyed pixie who obviously adored him. And didn't take him all that seriously.

"This place is really coming along," Ridge commented after a cool sip. "Kyle told me you're almost done."

Matt and Caty exchanged a look, then a smile. Ridge had the distinct feeling he was part of their joke. "What?"

"Nothing," Caty assured him. "The kids really like you, is all. It's nice."

"Speaking of kids, how do you like coaching?" Matt asked.

Grateful to be on male ground, Ridge grinned. "Awesome. Those kids are something else. I mean, they're not all headed for the pros, or even varsity, but they give it everything they've got. It's a kick to work with 'em."

"Well, Emily told me you're the best," Caty said. "Kyle thinks you're Vince Lombardi and Joe Montana rolled into one."

"Oh, man." Ridge grinned at Matt. "Your wife speaks football."

"I'm a lucky man."

Caty laughed. "We'll see how you feel later this season when my Panthers chew up your Falcons and spit them out."

"Hate to tell you," Ridge put in, "but the Broncos are the team to beat this year."

"In your dreams," Matt grumbled.

They bantered back and forth a while longer, but when Ridge caught Matt covering a yawn, he realized it was getting late. He was an early riser, but when he got up most mornings, Matt was already out in the fields.

"Well, I've got some early jobs tomorrow," Ridge said, standing up. "I should get to bed."

"Your package is on the entry table," Caty told him. "Matt said there are books inside, and I didn't want them getting any more dew on them."

"A fellow book lover," Ridge commented with a smile.

"Don't get her started," Matt warned. "You'll be here all night."

"I inherited a great collection from my grandparents, but I lost it when my old house burned down. I have a list of all the books, and I'm replacing them as I can find them."

"My grandfather has a friend in England who's a rare-book dealer." Ridge scrolled through his contact list and found the number. "His name's Edmund Collier. I'll text his info to you. If anybody can track down what you need, it'll be him."

Caty's eyes lit up as if he'd just offered to fly her around the world for free. "That's fabulous! Thank you."

"No problem." He hit Send and saluted her with his phone. "Good luck with it."

"I'll call him tomorrow," she said in an excited voice that made her husband chuckle.

"Wonderful. Thanks a lot, buddy."

"Anytime."

Matt and Caty exchanged one of those silent looks that couples attuned to each other seemed to use.

"I'll get your box," she said, moving past Ridge to go inside.

Ridge opened the door for her and turned to face Matt. "What?"

"That package is for Marianne, isn't it?"

Whoa. Ridge had forgotten how sharp Matt was. Trying to look casual, he shrugged. "I was chatting with Edmund and mentioned that I knew someone who used to have a first edition of *Little Women*. He got a set in recently, so I bought them for her. Y'know, to pay her back for all the food I've been eating."

"How'd you know she had them in the first place? Thinking about how they got ruined makes her mad, so she never mentions it." After a couple seconds, Matt leaned back and grinned. "Lisa told you."

"We were talking, and it came up."

"Right."

He dragged the word out on a skeptical drawl, but Ridge held his ground. He had his story, and shaky as it was, he was sticking to it.

Fortunately, Caty returned with his package then, and he took it from her.

"Thanks for taking such good care of this," he said, smiling down at her. "With any luck, Edmund will be sending you some of your own soon."

"That would be cool." Standing on tiptoe, she kissed his cheek. "I'm sure Marianne will love them."

"Were you listening in on us?" he asked.

Clearly insulted, she gave him a slanty-eyed look. "I'm not a moron, you know."

"That's true," Matt chimed in. "Hate to be the one to tell you, but you're pretty easy to read these days."

Totally busted, Ridge headed down the porch steps before stopping in the middle and looking back. "Do you think Marianne sees it?"

"Not a chance," Matt told him confidently.

"Why do you say it like that?"

"She doesn't want to see it. Ever again," he added with a frown. "If you're serious about this, you've got a lot o' work ahead of you."

"So why'd you set us up?"

He expected a denial, or some good old-fashioned stonewalling. Instead, his old buddy asked, "When did you figure it out?"

"At the wedding." Ridge grinned over at Caty. "I'm not a moron, either."

They all laughed at that, and Ridge headed down the steps again. Before tucking the very special package into one of the bike's saddlebags, he looked down at the box. Even though it wasn't very big, it had cost him a small fortune. But if his gift got him one of Marianne's amazing smiles, he'd consider it worth every penny.

Chapter Nine

On Wednesday, promptly at four, Peter's Jag came rolling down the driveway. Checking the mirror next to the door, Marianne plastered an uninterested but pleasant look on her face. He'd called earlier to tell her was leaving at six to get back to Charlotte for a supper meeting. She could tolerate him for two hours. At least, that's what she'd been telling herself all afternoon.

Kyle was at the kitchen table finishing his math homework, and he glowered through the screen door. "Two hours, right?"

Hearing her thoughts echoed in his resigned tone, she forced herself to sound upbeat. "Right. And it looks like he brought you something. Maybe you'll have fun today."

Angling his head, he gave her an I-don't-think-so look. "He can't buy me off with presents.

Caleb's dad tries that every time he visits, and it hasn't worked yet. Caleb sells the stuff online."

"He does not," Marianne protested. "He's only ten."

"Well, his mom does. They save up the money and take a trip. Last time, they went to Disney World."

Their discussion was cut short when Peter appeared in the doorway. Tucker stood like a statue in front of the door, growling like a small bear. Marianne grabbed his collar and let Peter in.

"You really should do something about that dog," he complained.

"Why? We trained him this way." Reaching down, she ruffled the Lab's chest with her free hand. "Good boy."

Tucker retreated to his braided rug in the corner, but even though he lay down, he kept a wary eye on their guest. Marianne knew just how he felt.

Clearly unsettled, Peter turned to Kyle. "When I was here last, I noticed you have a game system in the living room. One of my clients has a son your age, and we got to talking about what boys like these days." He held out a video game box. "He and his son have a lot of fun playing this."

Kyle's overly patient expression softened a little, and he took the box. "My friend Jimmy has this one. It's pretty good."

Not a ringing endorsement, but at least Kyle was trying to be nice. Marianne was torn. While she wasn't anxious for them to become best friends, she admired the character Kyle was showing in a difficult situation. If he was this composed now, she could only imagine how solid he'd be when he was older. It gave her great hope for his teenage years.

Emily had gone to a friend's house after school and wouldn't be back until suppertime. Her absence left Marianne in the awkward position of being a third wheel.

"There are snacks in the fridge, so help yourselves," she said as she moved toward the archway. "If you need me, I'll be in my office studying."

Peter didn't bother to ask what she was studying, which was a relief. She really didn't want to explain it to him.

Marianne half closed the door behind her so she'd be accessible, but wouldn't appear to be intruding on their visit. Once they got the game installed, Kyle guided Peter through the first level, giving suggestions on how to hold the controller and which paths were booby-trapped. Grudgingly, she had to give her ex-husband credit. He'd come up with something he and Kyle could do together that didn't require direct conversation. She heard them trading comments about this character and that obstacle, and she sighed.

Hoping to distract herself, she turned to her reading, scrolling back a page to pick up what she'd missed. Eventually, she decided it was pointless and gave up. As much as she hated to admit it, she was jealous. Kyle and his buddies played those games, and lately Ridge had joined their club. But she and Emily were told very firmly, "no girls allowed." It wasn't that the games were too hard, and Marianne always checked them out on a parents' video game website to make sure they weren't gory or filled with swearing.

No, she realized as she opened her top drawer to get a piece of gum. It was simply that her little boy was growing up. He didn't want to play games with his mommy anymore. Preoccupied by her thoughts, she almost didn't notice the package in her drawer. She pulled it fully open and found a box wrapped in pink paper covered with rosebuds.

Topped with a silver bow, it had no card. She took the box out and dug through the drawer, thinking the card had slipped underneath something. After a thorough search, she couldn't find one.

Curious, she ripped open the paper to find a beautiful white box embossed in gold with the words *Treasured Books, London, England.* Her heart pounding with excitement, she opened the hinged cover and looked inside.

There, nestled side by side in padded velvet frames, were two leather-bound books. They were the first and second volumes of *Little Women,* which had been originally published in two parts. She recognized the covers from the originals her father had given her when she graduated college. Her hands were trembling, and she wiped them off on her jeans before lifting out the first book. Turning to the title page, she gasped at what she saw.

For little Matilda. Your friend, Louisa May Alcott.

The ink had faded to a rust color, but "December, 1868" and the author's bold signature were still easy to read. Marianne couldn't imagine how much an autographed first edition Alcott was worth because she couldn't get her head around that many zeroes.

Which got her wondering who'd bought these for her.

Ordinarily, none of the Sawyers would have even considered buying something this extravagant. But their father's life insurance, held in trust for the past year, had just paid John, Lisa and Matt each a fairly hefty sum. She ruled out Matt, since every penny he and Caty had was going into finishing their house. As much as she adored her younger brother, she didn't think he had the connections to buy anything in London.

That left her very generous—and very dreamy—little sister. It would be just like Lisa to do something like this. Smiling, Marianne picked up the cordless phone and hit the speed dial for the diner.

"Ruthy's Place, Lisa speaking."

"You're the sweetest, most wonderful sister in the world."

"Gee, thanks," she answered, the antique cash register dinging while she punched the old buttons. "What did I do?"

"I found something in my desk just now," Marianne prodded.

"Honey, I didn't leave anything in your desk. After that printer fiasco, you banned me from your office. Remember?"

"Sure, but since when do you follow the rules?"

"Marianne," Lisa said in a serious tone, "that's your space, and you told me to stay out of it. What did you find?"

Marianne told her, and Lisa whistled in appreciation. "They'd be pretty pricey, wouldn't they?"

"Extremely. If it's not the boys and it's not you, I don't know anyone else with that kind of money."

"Maybe it's someone who doesn't have a lot, but thinks those books are worth the investment."

Judging by her tone, Lisa knew exactly who'd

bought them for her—but Marianne was stumped. "I don't know anyone like that."

Lisa laughed as if she'd just heard the best joke ever. "Look, I hate to do this, but a bus full of soccer players just showed up. Call me later if you want."

"Okay. Thanks, Lise."

"Love you."

"Love you, too."

After they hung up, Marianne stared at the elegant box and let her mind wander a little. No one outside her family knew about those books, how much they'd meant to her. Then it struck her.

Ridge.

Suddenly it all made sense. These were the books Ridge had picked up at Matt's. Lisa must have told him about Marianne's books getting ruined. From all those years of being a pilot, he probably had friends all over the world. He just might know people in England who could get their hands on rare classics like these.

Careful to make some noise, she got up and opened her door. "I need some water. Can I get you guys anything?"

"No, we're good," Kyle responded, leaning to the side to make a sharp turn on some kind of wacky trail. Peter looked completely engrossed in the game, so she kept going.

Through the kitchen window, she saw Betsy

parked on a tarp, pieces and parts spread around her as if she were being displayed at a flea market. Strains of classic rock music floated in on the breeze, and Marianne heard Ridge singing along with Aerosmith. He couldn't hit all of Steven Tyler's notes, she noticed with a grin, but he put a lot of energy into trying.

Marianne grabbed two water bottles from the fridge and headed outside. She left Tucker in the kitchen because she wanted Peter to know that he was still under surveillance. As she strolled out toward the antique plane, Ridge glanced up and instantly got to his feet. Not many men stood when a woman approached these days, she mused with a smile. Those old-fashioned manners were yet another pleasant surprise hidden beneath his less-than-polished exterior.

"Hey there," he greeted her with a smile. "What's up?"

Feeling shy all of a sudden, she held out a bottle as a buffer between them. "I thought you might be thirsty."

"I am. Thanks." He twisted off the top and took a long swallow. "How're things going in there?"

"Fine. Peter brought a video game for them to play."

Ridge chuckled. "Funny. I figured he was a take-no-prisoners Monopoly kinda guy."

His humorous attitude made her laugh. She'd

always dreaded Peter coming back at them like a nasty boomerang. Instead, he was proving to be more like a mosquito buzzing around her family. He was annoying, but she could handle him.

Comparing that to the sheer terror she'd felt seeing him at the diner, she recognized that something inside her had changed. Somehow, without realizing it, she'd regained the lion's share of her confidence. It gave her the strength she needed to go up against Peter rather than buckling under his domineering personality.

Since Peter had materialized, she'd begged God countless times to help her combat her very personal demon. As hard as she'd tried, she hadn't heard or seen anything to make her think her prayer had been answered. Now she realized He'd answered her, after all.

He'd sent her Ridge.

His steadfast support encouraged her to take chances, to stand up for herself, when not long ago she'd have done everything in her power to avoid a direct confrontation with her ex-husband. She owed Ridge so much, she didn't know how she'd ever repay his kindness.

"Thank you for the books."

The words came out so faintly, she felt ridiculous. She was a grown woman with two children, for goodness sakes. Why did she suddenly feel like a wallflower who'd been asked to the prom?

His hands full of grease from the gear assembly he was holding, Ridge just smiled. The sunlight accented the gold in his eyes, and his tanned face flooded with relief. Obviously, he'd been as uncertain about his gift as she was.

"It was an incredibly thoughtful thing to do," she continued with a smile of her own. "What made you think of it?"

He set down the grimy tool and wiped his hands on a cloth that was only slightly cleaner. "Well, I was talking with Lisa and she mentioned that your set got ruined. Grandpa knows this rare book dealer in London, so I called him up. He just happened to have them."

"Signed by Louisa herself. They must be worth a fortune."

Ridge shrugged, and she rested a hand on his shoulder. Broad and strong, those shoulders had taken on some of her worrisome burdens without her even noticing. When his eyes met hers, she felt an undeniable tug on her heart. It had happened a few times when she was with him, but she'd always ignored it.

This time, she didn't.

"You know what those books mean to me," she said. "How?"

"Your father gave them to you, and some careless idiot ruined them. When I heard about it, I got pretty mad. You must have felt even worse."

"And you wanted to make me feel better. That's just about the sweetest thing I've ever heard."

His gaze warmed, and he moved in closer. "I can be sweet."

"Really?" Deciding she'd enjoy the game he'd invited her to play, she gave him a mock frown. "I'll need some proof."

Leaning in, he brushed his lips over hers, giving her plenty of room to pull away. Instead, she moved closer, relishing the solid feel of him.

"I'm filthy," he murmured against her cheek.

"I don't care."

The moment Ridge took her in his arms, every last doubt she had about him simply melted away. Standing on that grungy tarp, wrapped up in the warmth of him, she thanked God for dropping this amazing man into her life.

It was the best money he'd ever spent.

To see that delighted look on Marianne's face again, Ridge knew he would do anything. That evening, Matt and John quit uncharacteristically early, and Caty and Lisa joined them for supper. They drove out to the farm together, loaded down with steaks and four different kinds of shish kebobs.

While the kids splashed around in the pond with

Caty, the guys fired up the enormous grill and got to work. Lisa and Marianne pegged bright red-and-white-checked cloths onto the longest picnic table and hung an electric bug zapper nearby. Tucker hated the thing, and he ran circles around it, barking every time it sizzled. With a mustard-colored harvest moon hanging low in the sky, it was the perfect fall evening.

Through the wonders of feminine coordination, all the food was ready at once. Everyone settled at the table, making sure to keep the meat platters in the middle where Tucker couldn't reach them. He could smell them, though, and his nose twitched approvingly as he sniffed the air.

"All right, Tucker, lie down," Marianne ordered, pointing behind the kids' bench with her salad tongs.

He gave her a pitiful look, and she repeated her command more firmly. Heaving a canine sigh, he dropped down and settled his chin on his paws. While Marianne was preoccupied cutting up Emily's steak, Ridge snuck a piece of rib eye to the pathetic Lab. Kyle gave him a look, and Ridge winked back. The kid grinned and continued his story about the field trip their class had taken to the local aquarium that day.

It was one of those moments lots of people had every day. The kind that flashed by so fast, they were easy to miss. But for someone like Ridge, they didn't come around very often. To him, this evening was priceless.

"I saw that," Marianne informed him as she began cutting up her own meat. "You're going to turn him into a beggar."

"Aw, he's a good dog." Ridge chopped his steak knife through his corn on the cob and tossed half of it to Tucker. "We all need a little treat once in a while."

Trying to look casual, he gave her a quick grin. When she blushed and looked away, he knew he'd made his point. They took their time over supper, filling and refilling plates, polishing off several gallons of sweet tea and lemonade. Even after the food had been cleared away, they lingered, talking and laughing.

"Y'know," Ridge said at one point, "the last time I had this much fun was your Fourth of July picnic. Before that, I honestly can't remember."

"Oh, Ridge." Emily patted his hand in her endearing way. "When you want to have fun, you should come here. We love you."

"You're just like a Sawyer," Kyle agreed.

From his seat at the end of the table, Matt said, "I always thought so."

As the others chimed in with similar comments, it struck Ridge that his untamable old buddy was the head of this warm, chaotic family. Matt had found his place—and his peace—in the last spot he'd probably expected. That they'd accepted Ridge as one of their own gave him the same feeling he'd gotten in church that first Sunday.

Harland was a place where he could belong.

He could quit roaming around and come in for a landing, right here in this town filled with friendly, welcoming people. There were apartments in town he could rent, and he'd be around to help out at the farm if they needed him. He'd always love flying, but it would be nice to have somewhere to come back to.

The only thing that could make it better would be to have a family waiting for him when he got there.

During all this, Marianne was unusually quiet. She was pushing peppers and tomatoes around her plate with her fork, completely withdrawn from the lively discussion. After their brief but heartfelt exchange that afternoon, her attitude concerned him. Having been so thoroughly betrayed in the past, she was understandably hesitant to embrace him completely.

But he wasn't giving up on her. Not by a long shot.

"Thanks, guys," he said when they left him an opening. "That's pretty cool."

"You're pretty cool," Kyle told him. Emily,

whose mouth was full of watermelon, nodded her agreement.

Ridge didn't know how to respond to that. It wasn't every day a big, loving family basically adopted you, and he didn't have words for how great it made him feel.

Fortunately, Tucker chose that moment to forget all the manners he'd ever learned. He ripped the cloth from the table with his teeth and took off with it, scattering food everywhere. With everyone laughing and chasing after him, it was the perfect end to a Sawyer family meal.

When they pulled in at football practice on Friday, Peter's Jag was already in the parking lot.

"What's he doing here?" Ridge muttered to Marianne.

Giving him a warning look, she looked in the rearview mirror. "Kyle, did you invite your father to watch you practice?"

"Nope."

Since he sounded totally unconcerned, she tamped down her own annoyance and forced cheerfulness into her tone. "Well, it was nice of him to come."

"I guess," her son muttered.

They all piled out of the van, and Emily took off like a shot to join the cheerleaders while Marianne set up her command post. When everything was in its place, she unfolded the extra-comfy portable papasan chair she'd splurged on. It would make sitting on the sidelines day after day much more pleasant.

Peter was in the stands today, head down as he thumbed away on his phone. When he glanced up and saw them, he raised a hand in greeting. Kyle returned the gesture before joining the game of keepaway that was already in progress. Ridge gave Marianne a look that clearly said "whatever," and headed for the bench.

Realizing that there was no way to make Peter go away, she settled down to grade papers. With her own schoolwork taking so much of her time, she used practices to stay on top of her teaching responsibilities. Today she was going through her students' handwriting assignments. A few were excellent, but most needed various suggestions for improvement. As she was working her way through the pile, her phone signaled a text message. Expecting it to be from Ridge, she frowned when the caller I.D. came up blank—dinner tonight? it said.

Anyone from Harland would call it "supper," and that clued her in to the sender. Marianne groaned out loud. Wasn't it bad enough that Peter had invaded her home and shanghaied Kyle's precious free time? Now he wanted to have a meal with her. She recognized the invitation for what it was: manipulation. He had something to discuss with her, and he wanted to take away any advantage she might gain by having him on her home turf. He was texting so he didn't have to face her. Coward.

Deciding to yank his designer chain a little, she typed: who is this?

peter.

busy. come talk now.

When he suggested a different night, she ignored the message and got back to work. She wasn't surprised when he appeared in front of her a few minutes later. It had rained earlier, and she was just annoyed enough to be pleased that he'd gotten mud on his shiny, tasseled loafers.

"What do you want, Peter?" she asked without looking up.

After a brief hesitation, he said, "I need to talk to you about Kyle."

"What about him?"

"Please look at me when I'm speaking to you."

Despite the polite phrasing, there was a commanding tone beneath the words that made Marianne long to do the exact opposite. Making him feel invisible might work for her, but it would only anger him, and then he'd make a scene. That would embarrass Kyle in front of his friends, which was the last thing she wanted.

Marking her place with her pen, Marianne looked up at him. "What about him?"

"I'm returning to Washington tomorrow morning, and I'd like to take him home with me."

Her back stiffened, and it was all she could do to stay calmly in her seat. "Not in this lifetime."

"Just for the weekend," he persisted, suddenly oozing charm. He hunkered down next to her chair and gave her a deceptively pleasant smile. "I think he'd love to see all the monuments and the Smithsonian, and the Redskins are playing on Sunday. He'd get a firsthand look at what real football is like."

"This *is* real football," she argued, motioning out to the field. "Their championship game is on Sunday. They need him."

"It's peewee football," he scoffed. "No one will miss him."

"Everyone would," Marianne argued. "Besides that, if you asked him, he'd say no. When he signed up, he committed to playing with his team at every practice and every game. He understands how important it is to keep his promises."

Peter's dark eyes glittered with something akin to approval. "Was that a dig?"

"Yes."

"Impressive." His thin-lipped smile made her think of a lizard. "You never used to do that, even when I deserved it."

"You can't charm me into agreeing to this trip," she shot back, eyes narrowed. "I said you could visit with Kyle at the farm. Don't push for more."

"A boy needs a father, don't you think?"

She unleashed the long, hard stare that still made her brothers squirm. "If that father is you, then no."

Clearly offended, which was her intent, Peter uncoiled and stood to look down at her once again. "You should reconsider your position on this. You'll regret making trouble with me."

"If you don't back off, you're gonna regret making it with me."

As usual, she hadn't heard Ridge approaching, but Marianne was delighted to hear his strong, I-mean-business voice. The light touch of his hand on her shoulder was so reassuring, she actually smiled at her ex-husband. "Goodbye, Peter. Have a good trip back to Washington."

Obviously furious at being outmaneuvered, he pointed a threatening finger at her. "This isn't over, Marianne. You can't keep me from my own son."

No, but I can keep him from you.

Those defiant words were on the tip of her

tongue, but she held back. She didn't want to say anything Peter could use against her later. Things between them had already deteriorated to a dangerous level, and she had a sinking feeling it wouldn't take much to make them worse.

"Would having him visit me once in a while really be so bad?" Peter asked in a wheedling tone she knew was designed to insult her intelligence. "I mean, you'd still have Emily."

"They're not a set of chairs," she pointed out, trying to keep her voice down. "They love each other, and they're used to being together. You can't split them up just because it happens to work for you."

She didn't dare mention her own feelings on the matter. She'd sooner rip off her arm than let Kyle go anywhere with his selfish, unpredictable father. It wasn't Peter's style to stop with simple overnight visits. If she gave in now, he'd railroad her into who knew what. Over the years, she'd come to realize that she'd never really understood him. That impression had grown exponentially in the last five minutes.

"That's your final word on this?" he taunted.

"Yes, it is."

His expression hardened. "Fine."

The curt response told her it was anything but fine, though she decided it was wise not to pursue it further now. They'd discuss it again, she was certain. Probably more than once before he eventually got the message that she wasn't changing her mind.

With a final glare at her and Ridge, Peter turned on his heel and stalked toward his car. Over his shoulder, he tossed the exact words she'd been dreading since he first showed up in Harland.

"You'll be hearing from my attorney."

After his car disappeared in a cloud of dust, Ridge leaned down to kiss the top of her head. "The kids and I can catch a ride home with Charlie. I think you'd better go see Caty."

Chapter Ten

It sure was handy having a lawyer in the family.

The thought popped into Marianne's head several times while she gave Caty the gist of every discussion she'd had with Peter during the last week. Always calm and reassuring, her sister-in-law listened carefully, asking a question here and there while she took notes. The rest of the house's interior was still in various stages of completion, but Matt had made sure Caty's office was the first room finished. He'd hung the heavy, soundproof door himself.

She and Marianne sat in comfortable chairs on opposite sides of an antique table that held their untouched tea and some of Ruthy's shortbread cookies. When Marianne was done speaking, Caty sat back with a frown.

"I'm not a custody expert, but this doesn't sound

good to me. You said Peter's brother will represent him in court?"

"Nick," Marianne clarified with a resigned nod.
"He represented Peter during our divorce, which
was the main reason I gave up on getting anything.
Peter has a top-notch trial attorney who works for
free. The only ones I found wanted way more than
I could afford," she added in a wry tone.

Caty smiled and made another note. "My friend
Jen in Charlotte handles tricky cases like this. She
got into custody law because her parents' divorce
split up her and her brothers."

"Do you trust her?"

Caty fixed her with a somber look. "Implicitly.
I'd love to help you, but I know very little about
this kind of law. Jen's the one you need. With you
and Peter living in different states, it could get
complicated."

"I don't care about the money he owes me,"
Marianne insisted. "But I'm not sharing custody
with a man who abandoned his own children."

"Of course not. I'm just saying that I don't know
if or how Peter's being in DC affects your case.
Jen will."

"My case." Marianne got light-headed as the
words buzzed in her ears. After a couple of deep
breaths, the feeling passed, but her anxiety kicked
up another notch. "If Nick pulls some strings and

gets him the right judge, Peter could win some kind of joint custody, couldn't he?"

"I wish I could reassure you, but the truth is I don't know. This kind of law is beyond me."

"Kyle barely tolerates Peter as it is," Marianne continued. "I can't imagine how he'll react if he's forced to spend time with his father on a regular basis."

Actually, she could, and none of the scenarios ended well. Tears welled up in her eyes, and she fought to keep them contained. She never cried because tears didn't solve anything. But now, years of worry rushed to the surface, and she was having a tough time keeping it together.

"Marianne, look at me."

Caty's firm but sympathetic tone got through, and she met Marianne's look of horror with a smile. "Stop trying to guess what's going to happen and call Jen. She won't charge you for a consultation, and she'll know what to do."

"I know from before how expensive this will be, and I don't have enough to pay her fees," Marianne confessed. "The money Dad left the kids is in trust, and I want them to have it when they're older. Other than that, all I have is the house."

"She's my friend, and we're family. We'll work something out."

Accustomed to handling problems on her own,

Marianne resisted what Caty was implying. She didn't want a handout from anyone, not even her big brother and his wife. There had been many days when she'd looked in the mirror and realized that the only thing she still possessed was her pride. If she lost that, what would she have left?

Her children.

The realization hit her with the emotional force of a hurricane, and she squared her shoulders, pushing aside all her doubts. Kyle and Emily were her world, and she'd do anything to keep her family intact. She wouldn't touch their inheritance, but she'd mortgage the house and hire Jen to get Peter out of their lives once and for all. If he were still alive, she knew her father would tell her to do exactly that.

It was just a house, she could imagine him saying, a collection of boards and windows that could be bought and sold many times over. Family was priceless.

The fact that she didn't even consider knuckling under brought Marianne a small measure of comfort. But this fight wouldn't be confined to just Peter and her.

"I can't stand the thought of the kids being dragged into court," she confided. "Will they have to testify?"

"Emily's a little young, and she's not part of the issue, so she's probably safe. Kyle, definitely," Caty added with a frown. "Based on his lack of contact with Peter, I'm sure the judge will want to get his opinion."

Closing her eyes, Marianne prayed for some kind of sign to guide her decision. She didn't get one, which told her she was on her own. She knew that meant God was confident she could handle it. She just wished she felt as certain.

"All right," she finally agreed, nodding to convince herself as much as Caty. "I'll talk to Jen. What's her number?"

Crossing the office to sit at her desk, Caty scrolled through the electronic address book on her laptop and wrote down the information for Marianne. As she handed over the slip of paper, she smiled encouragement.

"Try not to worry, Mare. We all love you and the kids, and we're in this with you. Anytime you want to talk, just let me know."

"You might regret saying that," Marianne warned as she took her purse from a hook by the door.

Caty responded with a warm hug, and Marianne gladly let herself be comforted.

Thank you, God, for giving me such a wonderful family.

* * *

"Thanks for the ride, coach."

Ridge lifted Emily from the car seat built into the back of Charlie Simmons's extended-cab pickup. Kyle slid out after her and closed the door.

"Not a problem," the man assured him. "Everything okay?"

"Sure. Marianne hadn't seen Caty in a while, so she drove over there to see how the house is coming along. You know how women get when they start talking."

Ridge had come up with that explanation earlier, and he was relieved that it seemed to satisfy everyone who asked. Except for Kyle, who hadn't said a word the whole way home. As Charlie pulled away, the kid was still sullen.

"Emily, why don't you go see what Uncle John's up to?" Ridge suggested. "Kyle and I have something to do in the barn."

"Okay," she agreed with that adorable smile. "Come on, Tucker. Let's go find Uncle John."

She skipped off toward the carriage house, the Lab trailing faithfully after her. Ridge's heart swelled with sudden, overwhelming emotion. Silently, he prayed for her to always be so sweet and carefree. He didn't want the world to intrude on her sunny view of life. He didn't know how he'd make that happen, but he wanted it with an intensity that amazed him.

For now, he turned to Kyle, hoping he looked calm and dependable. "Wanna talk about it?"

The poor kid sighed and stared down at his muddy cleats. "Not really."

Folding his arms, Ridge waited. He wouldn't force the boy to share what was bothering him, but he vaguely remembered being that age. If Grandpa stayed quiet long enough, making it clear he was ready to listen, Ridge would spill his guts. After a couple of minutes, his tactic was rewarded with the result he'd been hoping for.

Kyle looked up at him, misery filling his hazel eyes. "Mom's talking to Caty about my father, isn't she?"

Since he'd already figured it out, Ridge saw no reason to keep him in the dark. "Yeah, she is. She doesn't want you to know that, though, so keep it to yourself."

"She always worries about me. I wish she'd worry more about herself."

His tone and the words he chose got Ridge's attention. "What makes you say that?"

"I remember," he confided in a soft voice. "All he ever did was make her cry."

Ridge's heart just about stopped. He was no psychiatrist, but he had firsthand experience with the kind of situation Kyle had lived in back then. Marianne believed he'd been too young to understand.

She was wrong.

The boy lifted his head, and his eyes shone with tears Ridge knew he'd never shed. Kyle was his mother's son through and through.

"Can I talk to you about something?" Kyle asked.

"Sure."

Suddenly shy, he dug the toe of his cleat into the dirt. "It's about something I heard that I wasn't supposed to."

Thinking he'd heard some nasty words at school, Ridge casually settled on the bumper of John's car. "You can tell me anything, bud. Anytime."

"I think my father's trying to get money from Mom."

Every one of Ridge's hackles rose, and he suspected he looked like Tucker. Forcing calm into his voice, he asked, "What makes you think that?"

"I heard him on the phone earlier with some guy named Nick. They were talking about a company getting shut down by some general."

Sifting through what Marianne had told him about Peter's shady business practices, Ridge came up with something that fit. "The attorney general?"

"Yeah, that's it. He told this Nick dude he was working on a way to get him back his quarter mill." The poor kid didn't really understand what that meant, but he was smart enough to know it was bad. "He said Mom would sell the house to get the money for him so she wouldn't lose me."

So the stockbroker's hazy integrity had gotten him into a jam. It wasn't exactly a newsflash, but Ridge couldn't believe Peter had discussed his underhanded deal with Kyle anywhere nearby. Even worse, it was painfully obvious he wasn't really interested in his son. Or Marianne, although he seemed to enjoy taunting her.

Now that they knew what Peter was really after, they could keep him from getting it. The question was, how?

The sound of tires at the end of the driveway made them both look out toward the road. As Marianne's van turned in, Kyle cast Ridge a worried look.

"Don't tell Mom," he begged. "She'll get upset."

"I can't keep this from her." Ridge slid a reassuring arm around his shoulder pads. "We'll figure it out, though. I promise."

The fear in Kyle's eyes gave way to trust, and he nodded. That vote of confidence anchored Ridge a little more firmly to the family he'd come to think of as his own. When that had happened, he couldn't say, but it felt right somehow. Man, he thought with a grin. He really was a goner.

Marianne's van came down the lane, and they waited for her to park before walking over to join her.

"Is everything okay here?" Despite the worry clouding her eyes, her voice was as smooth as glass.

"Sure, Mom. I'm gonna get cleaned up for supper."

Giving her a quick hug, Kyle trotted inside, letting the screen door slam shut behind him. She turned to Ridge with a shocked expression.

"He hardly ever hugs me anymore. What was that all about?"

Ridge saw no point in hiding anything from her. "We had a little chat, is all. He's worried about you."

"That's my boy," she said with a proud smile.

Ridge's instinct was to give her a comforting hug, but he wasn't sure she'd respond well, so he held back. When she snaked her arms around his waist and squeezed tight, he wrapped her up in a full embrace.

"I'm right here," he murmured into her hair. "Everything's gonna be okay."

She responded to his reassurance the way Kyle had, Ridge noticed with pride. Nodding, she lifted her shoulders in a half sigh, half sob. Once she'd composed herself, she pulled her head back and gazed up at him.

"Caty's friend Jen specializes in custody law," she said. "I'm going to call her on Monday and hire her to end this nonsense with Peter for good."

Ridge had an idea of just how much courage it took for her to stand up to Peter, and he rewarded her with a quick kiss. "I think that's great."

"After that, I'm not sure." Frowning, she looked over at the old farmhouse. Light flooded from the windows, giving it a warm, homey appearance. "I'll have to mortgage the house, I guess. I hate to do it, but I don't have a choice."

Ridge hesitated. She needed to know what Kyle had overheard, but after the day she'd had, he wasn't sure how she'd take it. Then again, he hadn't gotten to be a freelance pilot by refusing to take a chance once in a while.

He kept his arm around her because he liked the way it felt. Steering her toward the picnic table nearest the pond, he asked, "If I say something you might not like, will you bite my head off?"

"Probably." Her quick smile told him she was kidding. "But go ahead. I just spent an hour with Caty discussing the Peter problem. My day's pretty well trashed anyway."

They both sat, and he rested his elbows back on the table, hoping the casual pose would ease some of the tension in the air. "The Peter problem," he echoed with a grin. "I like that."

"Caty came up with it," Marianne admitted with a wan smile. "She thought it made things sound less awful."

"She's right." Giving her an encouraging smile, he got to the point. "While you were gone, Kyle told me something."

He relayed the despicable plot Kyle had overheard, and noticed that she didn't look the least bit surprised.

"It sounds like one of Peter's investment schemes blew up in his face. Nick is his brother, not to mention his lawyer. That's why he has to get the money back."

"At your expense."

"Well, that's Peter."

Hearing her sound so dejected broke Ridge's heart, and he almost stopped the conversation right there. But he'd learned the hard way—more than once—that ignoring a problem didn't mean it went away. It just went into hiding, waiting to jump out and ambush you when you least expected it.

"There's something I don't get," Ridge said. "Why does he need money from you? That Jag he's driving is the $50,000 version."

"He's always been extravagant, and I'm sure he still spends more than he makes," she reasoned.

Why did a guy like that marry an innocent country girl? Ridge wondered.

"I wasn't always this jaded, you know," she said as if she'd read his mind. "When Peter and I met, I was more like Lisa. Sweet and trusting, full of big dreams."

The revelation got Ridge's attention, and he swiveled on the bench to face her. "What did you dream about?"

"Meeting a great guy, getting married, seeing the world."

He sensed that she was holding something back. Something important. "What else?"

When she hesitated, he knew he'd read her right. Because that had proven so hard to do, he felt like he'd scored a game-winning touchdown.

"Well, I used to enjoy writing." A faraway look came into her eyes, as if she was fondly gazing back at a simpler time in her life. "My favorite character in *Little Women* is Jo. I liked the way she decided to write and kept at it until she was good enough to publish her stories. I always thought it would be fun to do that."

"But?"

"Life happened," she admitted with a sigh. "I was busy with the kids and didn't have time for it anymore."

He heard what she wasn't saying and filled in the blank. "And Peter thought it wasn't important."

"I never mentioned it to him. I knew he'd think it was a foolish waste of time."

From her tone, he could tell that at some point during her marriage, she'd come to agree with her narrow-minded husband. Ridge took both of her hands in his, kissing one and then the other before connecting with the uncertainty in her eyes.

"Dreams are never foolish or a waste of time," he said gently. "They're what keep us going when things get tough, because we believe tomorrow will be better than today."

"My dreams are in there." She nodded toward the house where they could hear John and the kids laughing in the kitchen. "I wouldn't change that for anything."

"I know." Smiling, Ridge leaned in and kissed her. "But it's okay to have something just for you. It doesn't have to make sense to anyone else, as long as it makes you happy."

That got him a shy smile. "You make me happy."

His heart soared, and he barely smothered a triumphant howl. "I'm glad to hear that, 'cause you make me happy, too."

"And Kyle and Emily?" she asked in a hopeful voice.

He gave a mock growl. "Well, y'know, they

drive me nuts." They both laughed, and he added, "But they're great kids. I haven't had this much fun in a long, long time."

"Which do you prefer? Football or tea parties?"

"Can't I have both?"

"Oh, flyboy," she said with a rapidly warming smile. "That is so much the right answer."

She rewarded him with a long, grateful kiss that made him feel like Superman.

That evening, it was all Sawyers on deck. Marianne didn't call anyone, but somehow they all showed up just as she was putting supper on the table. John frequently ate with them, and it wasn't unusual for Lisa to stop by for a meal if she wasn't busy.

But when Matt and Caty pulled in, Marianne angled a suspicious look at Ridge. "You called them, didn't you?"

"Yeah, I did, because you should have your family around for something like this." Kissing her cheek, he whispered, "The kids are over at the Perkinses', so I figured it couldn't hurt. They're your family, Marianne. Let 'em help you."

Sighing, she pulled more dishes out of the cupboard. At least he was nice enough to set the table for her. Nobody seemed interested in their food, so she started the conversation. "Ridge found out something you all should know."

Clearly flabbergasted, they listened while he filled them in on the latest. She'd heard it all before, but it still made Marianne's blood boil. After all these years, Peter hadn't given up trying to take advantage of her. Only this time, he was using her love for Kyle against her.

Well, he was in for a rude shock, she vowed silently. This time, she wasn't going to tuck tail and let him trample all over her.

When Ridge was finished, Matt gave her a long look down the table. "So what's the plan?"

"What do you mean, what's the plan?" Caty demanded venomously. "Jen will shred this guy in court, that's the plan."

Meeting each set of worried eyes, Marianne said, "The problem is, Peter and Nick can fight me forever if they want to."

"You can have the money Dad left me," Lisa offered without even blinking.

"And mine," John added. "I don't need that Ferrari anyway."

They all laughed, and she appreciated him easing the tension. Matt and Caty exchanged a look, and Marianne cut them off before they could offer. "No, that's not how I want to do it. Dad left you that money for yourselves, not so we can buy off

some greedy moron who managed to invest someone else's money in the wrong company."

"Then where will you get it from?" Lisa asked.

Wanting to sound confident about her decision,
Marianne took a deep breath to steady her voice.
"I'll mortgage the house. With the acreage that
goes with it, I should be able to get enough."

Matt glared his opinion of that. "No."

"Yes," she insisted to cut him off at the pass.
He might be head of the Sawyer clan, but this was
her decision. "The house belongs to me, and Peter
is my problem. It's the only thing that makes any
sense."

"But you just started paying for your classes,"
Lisa argued. "How can you do that if you have to
pay for the house, too?"

"Alan gave me a raise when he hired me full
time." It was true. The raise wasn't big, but it
would help. "If I have to, I can take out a student
loan to help with college. If it gets Peter out of our
lives, I'll call it an investment," she joked, hoping
to lighten the mood.

She failed miserably. She hadn't thought it was
possible, but Matt's scowl darkened. "Dad would
hate this idea."

"Dad would've done it himself," John corrected
him quietly. "And you know it."

After some more debate, they all reluctantly

agreed that, under the circumstances, it was their best option.

"Now, about Peter." Always prepared, Caty took a small pad and pen out of her purse. "I'll draw up a legal agreement for him to sign, and I'll run it past Jen. After she emasculates him in court—" she paused for an evil grin "—Peter will agree to have no more contact with you or the kids. No visits, no phone calls, texts or smoke signals. Anything else?"

"Dropping off the face of the earth would be perfect," Ridge growled.

Caty added that to the list and circled it several times. "I can't guarantee that one, but I'll do my best." Smiling, she stood and headed for the door with Matt in tow. "I'll go home and get started."

That seemed to cue John and Lisa that it was time to go. After a round of hugs, they all went home. Alone with Ridge, Marianne couldn't help wondering if she was doing the right thing.

As if sensing her emotions, he settled his arms around her and drew her close. It was a comforting feeling, having those strong, capable arms wrapped around her. He didn't say anything, but the way he held her said he wasn't planning to let go anytime soon.

The idea both thrilled and terrified her. This man had literally fallen out of the sky and turned her world upside down. It wasn't the scenario she'd pictured so many times growing up, but she had to admit it had turned out even better. The fact that he so shamelessly adored her children only made him more of a hero in her eyes.

Still snuggled against Ridge, she tilted back to look up at him. "Peter's leaving in the morning. Maybe I should tell him I know what he's up to."

Frowning, Ridge shook his head. "I know it sounds crazy, but for now I think it's better to let him think you're buying into this fake custody battle."

At first she balked, fearing it would make her appear gullible. Then again, her ex had always thought of her that way. She could see the benefit of keeping him in the dark a while longer. "Let him believe I'm so rattled I'm not thinking straight. Good idea."

"I get 'em now and again." Leaning in, Ridge gave her a long kiss. "Like just then. That wasn't bad."

Mischief sparkled in his eyes, making her laugh. The worry that had been strangling her melted away, and in that single moment, she knew.

She was in love with him.

Completely unexpected, it was also the last thing she wanted. She'd struggled long and hard to regain her self-esteem and rebuild the pieces of her that had withered away during her disaster of a marriage. With her father and her brothers in their lives, Kyle and Emily hadn't suffered from the lack of a father.

Or had they?

Seeing her son with Ridge, hearing some of their "guy talk," she'd noticed a distinct change in Kyle. He stood taller, not because he'd grown, but because he had more confidence. He loved working on Betsy, learning about the tools and skills mechanics used to keep things running. He had a knack for it, Ridge had told her.

And Emily. Ridge generously endured tea parties and coloring marathons, had even played Candyland over and over one rainy afternoon. When the rest of them begged off a tenth game, he played three more until Emily finally decided she'd had enough. He listened to her as intently as he did Kyle, showing her the same respect he would an adult.

Over the past few months, Ridge had proven himself to be rock-solid when someone needed him. The football team and Danny Hodges's secret scholarship came to mind, and Marianne smiled.

"Something funny?" Ridge asked.

"Sometimes things don't work out the way you expect."

"Such as?"

"Such as us," she said, wondering how he'd respond.

Tilting his head, he gave her that crooked grin she'd come to adore. "There's an *us?*"

Marianne took a deep, steadying breath and waited for the warning bells to go off in her head. When she didn't hear them, she realized it was because her mind had caught up with what her heart had known for weeks now.

"I'd like there to be." She smiled at the astonishment in his eyes. "Is that what you want, too?"

"Definitely."

Typical Ridge, he didn't hesitate. He didn't waffle or dance around, looking for pitfalls that might spell trouble for them. By necessity, Marianne had become a "look, then proceed with great caution" kind of person. Now that she'd seen how deftly Ridge managed his life's twists and turns, she had to admit there was something exciting about leaping first and figuring out the details later.

"I know we'll have problems," she continued. "You don't really like being in one place, and the kids and I are settled here."

"We'll figure something out." Cradling her cheek in his palm, Ridge sealed his promise with a kiss. "Together."

"Together," she echoed with a smile. "I like the way that sounds."

"Yeah." He gave her a slow, lazy grin that warmed her from head to toe. "Me, too."

* * *

Saturday afternoon, Ridge knew he had some serious thinking to do.

The Wildcats had squeaked out a one-point win in their final regular season game and were going into the championships undefeated for the first time in twenty-seven years. The entire town was excited by the prospect of finally beating their rival, Kenwood, for the title. Folks stopped him everywhere he went, asking his opinion on this or that, suggesting plays they thought would help the team win.

Some ideas were reasonable, others were downright crazy. He was pretty sure some were physically impossible, but he took each one in the spirit in which it was intended. Thanking each of them for their interest in the team, he expressed his hope that they'd come by the game tomorrow to cheer the kids on. Admission was free, but if half of them showed up, the concession stand would set a sales record.

What Ridge needed was some peace and quiet to work through something that had been floating around in his head since supper last night. Knowing Marianne would be calling the bank about a mortgage Monday morning, he didn't have much time. He did his best thinking in the air, but it was too cloudy to take Betsy up. Instead, he borrowed Matt's bike and started riding, hoping to clear his mind enough to make the hardest decision of his life.

Once Kyle had told him about the attorney general getting involved in Peter's shady deal, Ridge knew he could take care of the Peter problem himself. Now that Marianne was planning to mortgage her house to fight the snake in court, Ridge wanted nothing more than to save her and Kyle the heartache that would undoubtedly come along with it.

He just had to get his head around the solution.

While he mulled it over, he wasn't going anywhere in particular, but somehow ended up in Harland's quaint town square. When he spotted Pastor Charles in front of his church pulling weeds, Ridge took it as a sign and turned into the lot.

Apparently, God figured he could use some help with this one, Ridge mused with a grin. Parking the bike, he strolled over to the garden. "Want some help?"

"I wouldn't turn it down." Dressed in his usual gray shirt and trousers, the plump man paused and wiped his balding head with a tie-dyed bandanna that looked out of place with his conservative clothes. "My daughter's," he explained, waving the bandanna.

Ridge grinned. "That figures."

"Although I do like all the colors," he went on. "Bright and cheerful."

"They sure are." Ridge grabbed a trowel and

started digging down to the roots of a large dandelion.

They worked for a while, chatting as they moved along the front of the church. When they stopped for some water, Pastor Charles sat on the steps beside Ridge.

"You didn't come here to help with these weeds," he began gently. "Is there something you wanted to talk to me about?"

Rolling his water bottle between his hands, Ridge stared down at it. He wasn't good at asking for help, and it wasn't coming easily to him now. But he'd found a haven of sorts in the little white church, and he knew that was partly because of this kind man with the understanding smile.

"I really like it here in Harland," Ridge began.

"And we like having you here. You're a good man who's always ready to lend a hand. You've been a wonderful addition to our town."

"I'm not sure how good I am. I have a chance to help someone I really care about, but I'm not sure I want to do what it would take."

The pastor frowned. "It must be serious."

"It means giving up something I love, which makes it tough."

"May I ask a question?" When Ridge nodded, the pastor continued. "Is it the thing that you love, or the memories it represents?"

Thinking he knew the answer right away, Ridge

opened his mouth, then slowly closed it. Grinning, he shook his head. "Y'know, you're a pretty smart guy."

"We all have our moments." He patted Ridge's shoulder gently and pushed himself up to stand. "I'd imagine you have a call to make. I'll leave you to it."

As the man strode around the corner of the church toward the side garden, Ridge couldn't help chuckling. Glancing up, he had to smile.

"You're pretty smart, too. Thanks for the help."

Chapter Eleven

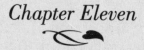

Early Sunday morning, Marianne was in the middle of packing the last cooler for the final game that started at noon. The sound of an approaching car caught her attention, and she saw an unfamiliar pickup park just short of Betsy's improvised landing strip. The driver and his older passenger stepped out, and Ridge strolled from the barn to shake their hands. They all chatted for a few minutes, then the younger man got back in the truck and headed to the highway. The older man handed Ridge an envelope and the two of them climbed the hill.

Through the screen, she heard him talking a blue streak, but almost nothing from Ridge. She couldn't make out any words, but the man's excitement intensified when they reached the plane. Running his hands along the metal body the way Ridge often did, he smiled in appreciation. He shook Ridge's hand again and, to her horror, started up the ladder fixed to the side of the biplane.

"No!"

The bag of ice she was holding burst when she dropped it, spewing ice all over the floor. Ignoring the mess, she raced out the door and toward the hill as fast as she could. Out of breath, she reached it just as the engine roared to life.

"Ridge, what are you doing?" she demanded, angrily watching the man go through his preflight routine. It was completely irrational, she knew, but for some reason she felt protective of the old plane. She didn't think Betsy should be going anywhere with any pilot but Ridge—who had the gall to look confused.

"Well, Ken's always had a hankering for a plane like Betsy, so I gave him a call."

"Why?"

As the dust whirled around them, Ridge handed over an envelope with his name written on it. In the upper left-hand corner was the imprint *Securities and Exchange Commission*.

Baffled, she looked at him for an explanation.

"Ken and I met in Alaska, when I flew him and his buddies up north for some elk hunting. They bagged three of 'em," he added with a maddening male grin. "Had to tie one to each wing to level out the plane."

Rolling her eyes, she snapped, "But what is this?"

When she waved the envelope at him, he grinned again. "Ken works for the SEC in Washington. After his great trip to Alaska, he said to call him if I ever needed a favor. When I told him I could use his help with a shady stockbroker, he was only too happy to oblige."

"What does Betsy have to do with this?"

"You don't get something for nothing," Ridge explained as if it were obvious. "In return for that," he nodded toward the letter, "I gave him Betsy."

Hands shaking, Marianne slit open the envelope and found a fully executed legal statement from Peter. In exchange for Ken not digging into his business, her ex had agreed to drop all current and future custody claims and never contact Marianne or her children again. It was the same result Caty had proposed, only Marianne wouldn't have to mortgage her house to get it.

But it was completely wrong.

"No." Pushing the papers against Ridge's chest, she pointed at the plane slowly rolling away from them. "Bring him back. Tell him you changed your mind."

"I'm not gonna change my mind." Taking her

hand gently, he pressed the priceless agreement into her palm. "I want to do this."

Out of the corner of her eye, she saw the plane moving more quickly now, preparing to lift off. *Ridge's dream,* was all she could think as Betsy gained speed and gracefully lifted into the cloudless morning sky. Silhouetted against the sun, it looked much the way it had the first time she'd laid eyes on it. Clearly wishing them farewell, Ken took the cheery blue-and-yellow biplane on a lazy loop around the farm, waving its wings before heading east.

Ridge watched in silence until the plane disappeared from view. His expression was unreadable, and Marianne felt absolutely horrible.

"How?" Because she couldn't begin to hold them back, tears streamed down her face as she looked up at him. "You loved that plane. How could you give it away?"

With a gentleness that amazed her, he took her face in his hands to brush her tears away with his thumbs. "I love you more."

Those beautiful words only made her cry harder, but she managed to say, "I love you, too."

"I didn't want you to mortgage your house. It's been in your family a long time, and it means a lot to all of you."

"But you and your grandfather worked on that

plane for years." While her tears had tapered off, she still couldn't understand his reasoning. "What will he think?"

"When I talked to him yesterday, he thought it was a logical solution to the Peter problem. Besides, you should've seen Ken's face. He's like a kid who woke up Christmas morning and found a puppy under the tree."

Whether Ridge truly believed everything he was saying or not, Marianne recognized that he'd thought it through and was content with his decision. This man's generosity was so endless, she couldn't believe it was for real.

"Are you sure about this?" she asked.

"Ken will take good care of her, and he'll have a blast flying her around to the shows."

Ridge had dodged her question, which was totally unlike him. "Right, but how do you feel about that?"

"I'm good with it," he said as he steered her toward the house. "Maybe someday I'll get another plane. Right now, we've got a big game to play."

Pulling him to a stop, she gazed up at him and smiled. There was really no way to properly thank Ridge for the tremendous sacrifice he'd made for her family.

Marianne prayed the kiss she gave him would be a start.

* * *

Championship Sunday started in church.

As a special treat, Pastor Charles had asked everyone to come dressed in their Wildcats gear. The fans took his suggestion to heart and wore their best blue and gold. The kids were quite a sight, with all those shoulder pads and pompoms jammed into the old wooden pews. After a quick sermon, he said a prayer for everyone to be safe during the game.

Then he slipped on his own Wildcats cap and motioned to the organist. The congregation filed out, accompanied by the rousing Notre Dame fight song. Marianne couldn't recall ever hearing something like that in church, and she flashed a smile at the inventive pastor. Grinning back, he escorted his wife and younger children down the aisle. Outside, everyone formed a long caravan of honking cars that headed out to the field.

It was a hard-fought game between Harland, last year's runners-up, and the Kenwood Mustangs, the defending champions. As the final seconds ticked away, Charlie called his last time-out. Huddling with his coaches and players, he turned to Ridge.

Reading his lips, Marianne saw him say, *Whatcha got?* Ridge's back was to her, so she didn't catch the response. Everyone in the circle let out a whoop and jumped up and down, obviously excited by whatever he'd suggested.

As they lined up, she heard the quarterback yelling out the play, "Betsy! Betsy! Betsy!"

Oh boy, she thought with a grin. This one must be a doozy.

Her heart in her throat, Marianne stood, along with half the population of Harland. More nervous than she'd ever been, her eyes went from the shifting formation of players to the clock. Five seconds. Three seconds. Finally, the center snapped the ball to the quarterback. For better or worse, this would be the last play of the game.

Chaos erupted everywhere as the young quarterback looked for his two receivers standing twenty yards away. They were waving their hands, which made the Kenwood coaches and parents yell, "It's a pass!" Four Kenwood defenders scattered downfield to block a throw. Marianne didn't know much about football strategy, but even she understood that meant there were four fewer players on the line.

Suddenly, there was a lot of hollering at the line of scrimmage, but it was too late. A fierce skirmish broke out on one side, as Kyle and Elisa Franks teamed up to make a hole. Danny Hodges grabbed the ball from the quarterback's hands and darted through the opening before any of the Mustangs could react.

Running like the thoroughbred Ridge had compared him to months ago, Danny flew forty yards down the sideline and into the end zone. Marianne didn't think his feet touched the ground until they crossed the goal line.

The hometown crowd erupted with joy, screaming to the players and hugging each other in the stands. The fence kept them off the field, but they rushed down to circle it, shouting their approval to the kids and coaches.

As the team mom, Marianne was allowed in with the players, and today she took full advantage of that privilege. One of the assistants opened the gate for her, and she raced through, sweeping her son right off his cleats. And for once, he didn't scold her for doing it.

"We won, Mom!" he crowed, hugging her ferociously. "We did it!"

Her throat clogged with pride, she laughed. "You sure did. You guys were awesome!"

He hugged her again, then slid down to jump onto the pile of players stacking up midfield in a group celebration. Concerned about Emily getting trampled in all that mayhem, Marianne was relieved to find her little cheerleader assistant safely perched on Ridge's shoulders. It seemed like a fitting picture, since he'd taken so much of Marianne's burden on those wide shoulders of his.

Still a romantic, she chided herself with a sigh. After being pragmatic for so long, it was actually nice to know she hadn't lost all her dreaminess.

"We won, Mommy!" Emily cheered, waving her honorary pompoms over her head. "Wasn't Danny great?"

"They were all great." Mindful of the people around them, Marianne kept her victory kiss under wraps and settled for giving Ridge a smile. "Was that your ace-in-the-hole play?"

Eyes sparkling with delight, he grinned. "Yeah, but the kids made it happen. Kenwood never saw it coming till it was too late."

Marianne noticed someone coming up beside her, and greeted Pamela Hodges. "Pam, you must be ecstatic. Your son's a bona fide hero."

"It's this man who's the hero." Her weary features lit up as she beamed at him. "You were right about the team, Coach Collins. It's done wonders for Danny."

"He's done wonders for us." Ridge gave her a warm smile. "And it's Ridge."

Off to the left, a chant of "MVP, MVP" started up, and the team lifted Danny onto their shoulders to carry him around the Wildcat painted in the middle of the field. Covering her mouth with her hand, Pam choked back a sob.

Marianne put an arm around the timid woman's shoulders. "It's okay. I feel the same way."

"God bless you," she whispered, gratitude mixing with the tears in her eyes as she glanced from Marianne to Ridge. "God bless both of you."

Patting Emily's leg, Marianne looked out to where Kyle was still celebrating with his teammates. Then she snuck her arm around Ridge and smiled up at the generous man who'd made it all possible. "He already has."

After quite the celebration at Ruthy's, Marianne finally got her crew home and cleaned up. The kids were wired, bouncing from one thing to the next. Knowing they'd get tired—eventually—she just let them run. It had been a wonderful day for everyone, and for once she had no intention of trying to reimpose order. Maybe, she thought as she piled whipped cream on four sundaes, Ridge's easygoing attitude was beginning to rub off on her.

Not long ago, the idea of it would have horrified her. Now it appealed to her tremendously.

"Here you go," she announced, placing a different mix in front of each. "Fudge for Kyle, strawberry for Emmy, caramel for me, and the works for Ridge."

While they spooned their way through the sweet layers, they talked about the game and how much fun they'd have at school tomorrow. Charlie had given the team permission to wear their game jerseys on Monday—dirt, sweat and all. Marianne was glad her students were too young to have played today. She could only imagine how those other classrooms would smell. After a few minutes, Ridge set his spoon down and crossed his arms on the table.

Looking at each of them, he said, "I have something to ask all of you."

His somber look was very much at odds with the playful twinkle in his eyes, and Marianne wondered what on earth was going on in that unpredictable mind of his. Normally, she was fairly patient, but his opening had made her a little anxious. "What is it?"

"Well, it's the end of the season for the farm and football. I've been thinking about what I should do this winter."

"You should stay here," Emily piped up.

"That's not up to us," Marianne reminded her gently. "Ridge can go where he wants."

The only problem with that was, she was in love with him. If he left, she honestly didn't know what she'd do.

Leaning forward, he fixed Marianne with an intense look that made her heart miss a beat. "What if I wanted to stay here and work on the farm? I could officially be part of the family and help you keep all this going. What would you say?"

"On the farm?" Kyle repeated. "With us?"

Still focused on Marianne, Ridge nodded. "If you'll have me."

Stunned beyond words, she needed several seconds to find her voice. When she did, it came out in a breathless squeak. "What are you saying?"

A lazy grin drifted across his sunburned face, and the most maddening man she'd ever met went down on his knee beside her.

"Marianne." Taking her hand, he looked over at her children. "Kyle and Emily. I love you more than I ever thought I could love anybody. Will you all marry me?"

The kids went bonkers, Emily squealing with delight while Kyle danced around the table, hugging everybody, including Tucker. Mimicking their reaction, the crazy Lab raced around barking and ended up with his paws on the table, panting with excitement.

Everything felt like it was swirling around her while Marianne stared at Ridge in disbelief. She hadn't dared to let herself even consider his staying, much less proposing. As always, he'd managed to catch her by surprise, and the ease with which he did it amazed her.

The fun-loving pilot had taken over her quiet little life and flipped it in a full barrel roll. By turns, he'd infuriated her, encouraged her, loved her even when she'd stubbornly pushed him away. Faced with his unexpected proposal, she tried to remember why, exactly, she'd sworn off men.

In the end, she gave up and started laughing. Dangling her arms over his shoulders, she leaned in and gave him a long, grateful kiss.

Cocking his head, he grinned. "Is that a yes?"

"Definitely."

* * * * *

Look for Mia Ross's next Love Inspired novel, A GIFT OF FAMILY, available in December.

Dear Reader,

This story has been kicking around in my imagination for a long time, just waiting to be told. Whether or not you can relate to Marianne, I hope you find inspiration in her decision to let go of the past and embrace the future.

Too often, we women are so busy taking care of others, we put ourselves at the bottom of our own to-do list. I'm glad you carved a few hours out of your busy days to read Marianne and Ridge's story. I'd be even happier if you made a habit of taking time to do things simply because you want to. We all deserve a little "me" time.

If you'd like to stop by for a visit, you'll find me online at www.miaross.com, and on Facebook and Twitter. While you're there, send me a message in your favorite format. I'd love to hear from you!

Mia Ross

Questions for Discussion

1. Marianne pretty much dislikes Ridge on sight. As she gets to know him, she gradually changes her mind. Have you experienced something like this with anyone you know?

2. Because of her failed marriage, Marianne is hesitant to get involved with any of the men her friends suggest to her. Are you or someone you know like that?

3. Marianne and Ridge have very different personalities. He's a free spirit, and she's not. Do you think people are born with those qualities or do they develop them?

4. Marianne's kids are her entire world, and she often forgets to take time out for herself. This happens to caregivers in many different circumstances. Can you think of ways for them to take care of themselves, too?

5. Ridge's father abused both him and his mother, which made him very protective of her, and later of others. Can you think of events in your own life that have shaped your behavior later?

6. Kyle is very grown-up for a ten-year-old. Do you know any children like that? Why do you think they've matured so quickly?

7. Emily gets attached to Ridge very quickly. Do you know any men who've stepped in to take the place of a child's absent father? Why do you think they take on that responsibility for a child who isn't their own?

8. Because of his own background, Ridge recognizes the signs that Marianne was emotionally abused by her ex-husband. Do you know anyone like that? Does she hide the truth or explain it away?

9. When Ridge realizes that Marianne no longer trusts her own judgment, he tries to boost her confidence by buying her a gift to remind her of better times. If you could return to a different time in your own life, when would it be?

10. Marianne envies her sister, Lisa, who's still a dreamer. Do you think it's possible to hang on to our dreams as we get older?

11. When Ridge talks to the pastor about giving up something he loves to help Marianne, the pastor suggests that it's not the object he loves,

but the memories it represents. Do you own anything like that?

12. Many of Ridge's good family memories are of him and his grandfather restoring Betsy. Can you think of experiences you could share with your children or grandchildren that would hold the same kind of meaning for both of you?

LARGER-PRINT BOOKS!

GET 2 FREE LARGER-PRINT NOVELS PLUS 2 FREE MYSTERY GIFTS

Love Inspired

Larger-print novels are now available...

LILP11B

SUSPENSE

RIVETING INSPIRATIONAL ROMANCE

Watch for our series of edge-
of-your-seat suspense novels.
These contemporary tales
of intrigue and romance
feature Christian characters
facing challenges to their faith...
and their lives!

AVAILABLE IN REGULAR
& LARGER-PRINT FORMATS

For exciting stories that reflect traditional values,
visit:
www.ReaderService.com

ReaderService.com

You can now manage your account online!

- Review your order history
- Manage your payments
- Update your address

We've redesigned the Reader Service website just for you.

Now you can:

- Read excerpts
- Respond to mailings and special monthly offers
- Learn about new series available to you

Visit us today:

www.ReaderService.com